PETE'S GOLD

OTHER BOOKS BY
LUANNE ARMSTRONG

Blue Valleys: An Ecological Memoir (Maa Press, 2007)

Breathing the Mountain (Leaf Books, 2003)

Into the Sun (Hodgepog Books, 2002)

The Bone House (New Star Books, 2002)

Jeannie and the Gentle Giants (Ronsdale Press, 2001)

Maggie and Shine (Hodgepog Books, 1999)

The Colour of Water (Caitlin Press, 1998)

Arly and Spike (Hodgepog Press, 1997)

The Woman in the Garden (Peachtree Press, 1996)

Bordering (Gynergy Books, 1995)

Annie (Polestar Press, 1995)

Castle Mountain (Polestar Press, 1981)

PETE'S GOLD

Luanne Armstrong

RONSDALE PRESS

RONSDALE PRESS
3350 West 21st Avenue, Vancouver, B.C., Canada V6S 1G7
www.ronsdalepress.com

Typesetting: Julie Cochrane, in Minion 12 pt on 16
Cover Art and Design: Nancy de Brouwer, Alofli Graphic Design
Paper: Ancient Forest Friendly "Silva" — 100% post-consumer waste,
    totally chlorine-free and acid-free

Ronsdale Press wishes to thank the following for their support of its publishing program: the Canada Council for the Arts, the Government of Canada through the Book Publishing Industry Development Program (BPIDP), and the Province of British Columbia through the British Columbia Book Publishing Tax Credit program and the British Columbia Arts Council.

Library and Archives Canada Cataloguing in Publication

Armstrong, Luanne, 1949–
    Pete's gold / Luanne Armstrong.

ISBN 978-1-55380-059-0

    I. Title.

PS8551.R7638P48 2008   jC813'.54   C2008-900946-0

At Ronsdale Press we are committed to protecting the environment. To this end we are working with Markets Initiative (www.oldgrowthfree.com) and printers to phase out our use of paper produced from ancient forests. This book is one step towards that goal.

Printed in Canada by Marquis Printing, Quebec

This book is dedicated to
Gaelin Armstrong Macdonald

ACKNOWLEDGEMENTS

With thanks for their help and
support to Dorothy Woodend,
Mary Woodbury, Jane Silcott,
and Ellen McGinn.

Chapter One

—

The muscles in Pete's shoulders flexed and expanded as he leaned forward, lifted the oars, leaned back and pulled with all his strength. The white rowboat leapt over the flat, dark-green water. Pete rowed hard for several minutes, then paused to breathe and stare around him. He could see the curve of beach he had left behind, and above it, a ragged blue-green fringe of trees. To the south, he could see a few cabins scattered above the rocks that made a serrated grey edge along the water. Above them, the mountain loomed like an enormous green-feathered wing.

The sun pulsed onto his neck and bare arms. He shook

his fingers to loosen them, and then started rowing again. His back was sore from the long bus ride from the city, and it felt good to stretch, to push his feet against the bottom of the boat. Now that he was past the long point of steep rocks that stretched out from the beach, he turned the boat so he could see the blue mountains marching northward on the other side of the lake.

The reflection of the mountains shimmered and shook into pieces as a wind came skipping across the water and blew pleasantly over his hot face. The wind smacked into the bow of the boat and shoved it sideways. The black and white collie dog standing in the bow of the boat lurched and almost fell, and then it leaned out over the water and began barking at its own reflection in the water. The dog was his grandmother's. It had followed him to the beach and had jumped into the boat as soon as Pete shoved it into the water.

Pete leaned over to see what the dog was staring at. All he could see was his own wavering reflection in the water, brown hair falling over his forehead, brown eyes, round freckled face.

Dancing lights from the water dazzled his eyes, and he lifted his head to stare around himself again. The lake was huge, nothing like the small lake near Victoria where he had learned to row. He looked across to the steep blue mountains on the other side. He wondered how far it was, if people ever went over there.

He started rowing again. Lean forward, dip the oars, pull and lean back, just as he had learned in summer camp. But the wind made rowing tricky. The boat swung one way, and then the other. One oar blade clipped the top of the water and bounced. The end of the oar jumped out of Pete's hand; the metal oar holder slipped out of the oarlock on the side of the boat and the oar slid into the water.

Pete stared at the oar. Then he looked at the dog.

"Fetch," he said, pointing. The dog ignored him. It kept running from one side of the boat to the other, staring into the water, rocking the boat and barking. "You stupid dog," he yelled. "Shut up." The dog ignored him. Suddenly Pete stopped rowing. His hands froze on the oars. Was there something down there, a shadow, something blacker than the black water, something huge? He tried to stare past the surface of the water but it kept shifting. It was like peering into a kaleidoscope. He lifted his head and looked around again. He suddenly realized he was a very small dot on a large lake. The mountains loomed over him like giants, laughing at this boy out on the water with no hat, no life-jacket, who didn't even know how to row a boat properly. The distance between the oar and the boat was rapidly increasing. He had better do something or he was going to have to make it back to land with only one oar.

He looked at the row of blank windows in the cottages and thought about waving for help. Was anyone looking? Would they think he was just some fool kid messing around in an old boat? Well, he was thirteen. He could look after himself.

He slipped off his sneakers and his new jeans, bought for the trip, then his black t-shirt. He stood up, balancing awkwardly in the tippy boat. He stepped up onto the seat, took a deep breath and dived into the water.

The cold raced like blue fire all over his skin, and into his blood. As soon as he surfaced, he opened his mouth and began gasping for air. He thrashed towards the oar, grabbed it and turned back to the boat. But the boat, lighter without his weight, and pushed by the wind, was drifting away from him as fast as he could swim.

The cold was really hurting, his skin was on fire and the top of his head felt like it was going to blow off. He hadn't realized that the lake in early summer would still be this cold. He swam harder. He was making it; the boat was coming closer, then another puff of wind skipped out of the sky and shoved it away from him again. But this time, the boat swirled around in a slow circle, and the piece of yellow plastic rope, hanging from the front, eddied towards him. He splashed towards it, kicking frantically, trying to hold the oar with one hand and swim hard with the other. Finally, with a last desperate lunge, he got his fingers on the very end of the rope, and pulled it closer. Now he could tread water and pull the boat towards him. The collie was looking down at him, wagging its tail. When he was next to the boat, he threw the oar over the side. He tried to lever himself in over the side of the boat but it was too tippy. He had

to swim around to the back of the boat, s
over the back and then slither over. He co
boat, his chest heaving, his body shaking wi
sun felt wonderful on his burning skin. When the dog came
over and licked his face, he opened his eyes, and then realized that the wind was growing even stronger now. Small
waves were rocking the boat and the wind was blowing it
faster and faster out towards the middle of the huge lake.

He figured he had to get back to shore before the wind
became even stronger. He settled himself on the seat, slipped
both oars back in the water and began rowing. The wind
slammed into the boat and spun it sideways. He had to pull
hard on one oar to straighten out. It was difficult to keep the
boat straight. A big wave surged towards the boat, which
climbed up one side of the wave and then slapped down
into the trough. Water slopped over the side, into the boat.
The wind slapped at his face, swirled against his ears. Fear
thrilled up from his belly into his throat. He rowed harder
and faster. Lean forward, dip the oars, pull, do it again,
faster, faster. C'mon, keep going, he said to himself. He kept
trying to look over his shoulder to see if the beach was
coming closer, but every time he did, he lost his rhythm, so
finally he just concentrated on rowing as hard as he could,
trying to keep the boat going straight. Inch by inch, he
maneuvered the boat closer to shore, even though it was
now climbing to the top of each wave and then crashing
into the trough before the next one.

Finally he was within the shelter of the long rocky point

t jutted out beside the beach, and the wind and the waves stopped trying to push him away. It was a lot easier rowing in calmer water.

His arms and shoulders were really hurting now. Wearily, he managed to row the boat to the beach where it grated on the sandy bottom. He jumped out, grabbed the rope at the front and pulled the boat up on the sand.

It was only then he noticed that his grandmother was sitting quietly on a log on the beach.

"Thought you might be in trouble there for a minute, but you handled it," she said.

Pete shrugged, embarrassed that she had caught him. He could feel his arms shaking from the effort of rowing so hard. His face burned. He expected her to lecture, maybe threaten him with grounding or something. Instead, she was smiling all over her face like some kind of old loony.

"Did you see the lake monster?" she asked, and laughed. "Supposed to be one. Lots of people have seen it."

Pete stared at her. He was way too old to believe in those kinds of silly stories.

"Water's kind of cold right now," she said, "but it will warm up soon. Or there's fishing. Do you like fishing?"

"I dunno," he mumbled, staring at his feet.

"Well, I'd better get back to the house. Got stuff to do. You coming?"

"Guess so," he said. All the way back up the hill, he thought about that strange shadow he'd seen under the boat. He would have liked to talk to her about it but the words stuck in his throat. Instead, he went into the house and lay on the creaky double bed in the room that was his for the next few weeks. He stared at the ceiling until he fell asleep, and then was wakened by his grandmother calling him for supper.

Chapter Two

—

Everything here smelled and sounded strange, Pete thought. The morning sun glared in the uncurtained windows. There were birds under the eaves of the house. He could hear them squeaking or squawking or whatever it was birds did. A rooster crowed in the yard. Suddenly Pete jumped. A squirrel had plunked onto the windowsill and was staring at him. The squirrel rattled some kind of weird squirrel talk at him. Probably telling him to get lost. Pete turned over and buried his face in the musty pillow. The blankets smelled old and dusty, as if they hadn't been washed in a while. Yuck. He had noticed the funny smell of the house when he first came in, yesterday morning.

He had been here one day and he was already so bored he could feel his brain shriveling. Plus he had been an idiot yesterday. A lucky idiot. He was glad no one knew about what had happened. Except his grandmother.

How was he going to survive the summer like this?

The floor creaked. His grandmother came to the doorway.

"Want some breakfast?" she asked.

"Nope." It came out more like a grunt. He didn't look at her, just kept his head in the pillow.

"Want to go to town and play video games?" she asked.

He took his face out of the pillow and stared at her.

She was laughing. Then she sat down on the bed and sighed.

"Look, sweetie, when you were little, you loved to play Lego. So we played Lego. Then you went through a period when you wanted to be a soldier, then an astronaut, then a policeman. I used to buy you toy guns, which made your mom so mad. Remember that time I bought you that crazy rocket ship and it blew up? Your poor mom. Having me around always drove her crazy."

Was that true? He remembered his mom saying that his grandma was different from most people.

"Pete, this wasn't my idea, you coming here for a visit but I want you to know I'm really glad you did. I hope we can have some fun together. But I don't know what you like anymore. You'll have to tell me."

Pete couldn't think of what to say. He wanted to say, just

send me back to the city and leave me on my own, but instead he kept staring at the ceiling, wishing she would go away and just leave him alone.

And after a while she stood up and left. Pete lay still. He had probably hurt her feelings by being so rude. He hadn't meant it. He was just so angry about everything. He turned over again and buried his face in the pillow. Images from the past few days flickered behind his eyes.

—

Was it really only yesterday morning that his grandmother had picked him up at the small dusty bus station in a small, dusty town that he knew he had seen before but couldn't really remember? The night on the bus had been so incredibly long and painful. He had tried all kinds of positions to sleep but none were comfortable.

When the bus finally pulled up at the one-room bus station in the dawn light, he had stomped down the bus steps to find his grandmother was waiting. Her face lit up when she saw him. She came towards him with her arms outstretched but he'd managed to avoid her. He mumbled hello and then he went and stood beside the bus while the driver unloaded the luggage and his grandmother signed the form the bus driver had held out, stating that she was his grandmother and would look after him. Then he climbed in her ancient green truck, holding his suitcase on his lap to keep it away from the dusty floor. They drove through the little town, past the 7-Eleven and the A&W, and then down another endlessly long road lined with forest and the occasional farm, until they reached her farm. Neither of them said much. His grandmother asked a few questions about the trip and his parents; he mumbled answers and then he put his head back and closed his eyes.

When he and his grandmother got out of the truck, he had followed her into the old farmhouse that he barely remembered from previous visits. She had shown him his room and he had thrown his suitcase on the bed. The bed sagged in the middle. There was no stereo, no television in his room. Did his grandmother even have a computer? How would he talk to his friends without email? He already missed his computer. Whenever he got bored, it was there to play with. His parents could have at least bought him a laptop to bring along. They could afford it.

He had sat on the bed for a bit and looked out the window at the sunny quiet yard. Then he had gone out to the kitchen where his grandmother was sitting at a round wooden kitchen table, drinking tea, reading and listening to the radio. There was a giant black cat on her lap and another grey one in the chair. The black and white collie under the table wagged its tail. His grandma's grey hair was cut very short. She was wearing a really ugly black sweatshirt.

He slumped into a chair. She closed the book and smiled at him. Her smile was too forced, too anxious.

He didn't smile back. The radio was playing something completely annoying, some classical junk.

"Would you like some breakfast?" she asked. "Toast, cereal, jam, tea, coffee? You'll have to tell me what you like. It's been a while since I had a boy to feed."

"Not hungry," he mumbled.

"Okay then. Suit yourself." She sighed, stopped smiling and went back to her book.

He didn't feel like eating in this cruddy old kitchen. The floor was covered with some brown stuff. The stove looked like it was a million years old. He didn't want to sit here and try and make conversation, something he was no good at.

"Maybe I'll go outside," he had said. "Look around."

"Okay," she said without looking up from her book. "Feel free."

There was an old picnic table outside on the shaggy lawn. The dog came outside with him, sniffed his feet, peed on the table leg and lay down on the grass, panting. The sun was already hot. It was going to be a long, hot, boring chunk of his precious summer with a grandmother he barely knew. When he was little, he had really liked her. He remembered that much. She used to come and visit a lot. She used to get down on the floor with him, build forts out of Lego, or play space wars. They used to have so much fun. She was always laughing and willing to try crazy things. But he hadn't seen her for the past few years. He didn't feel as though he really knew her anymore.

What was he doing here? At thirteen he should be hanging out in the mall with his friends, not stuck here in the country. What a stupid age thirteen was. Too young to live alone or run away, too old to be a kid, have tantrums, lock himself in his room, and hold his breath until he turned blue. Too young to be in charge of his own life because, if he was in charge, no way would he be stuck here because his parents had decided that in some insane way, this forced summer vacation would be good for him, give him some time to think, as his mother had said. Actually, he thought, they just wanted to get him out of the way so they could go on with their now-separate lives. He was just a nuisance.

Every time he thought about his parents, he felt mad and sick all over again. First, out of the blue, they dumped the information about their "trial separation," as his mom called it. Then they dumped him. Too busy with their careers to care about how he felt.

His grandmother came out of the house.

"I bought some chocolate doughnuts yesterday," she said. "They're on the table."

He stared at her.

She trudged past him, trailed by the dog and both cats.

"Got to feed things," she said. "Chickens . . . baby chicks, if you want to see."

Chocolate doughnuts. For breakfast? His mom would have a fit. Well, actually, now that she had mentioned it, he was really hungry. He went back in the house. There were chocolate doughnuts on the table along with a tall glass of milk, a plate with slices of watermelon, a bowl of raspberries and a package of pepperoni sticks.

He ate it all, and then went back outside, still chewing on some pepperoni. He sat back down at the picnic table. The sun beat down on his head. If his mother were here, she'd make him put on a hat and sunscreen, and carry a bottle of water.

His mother and father were both far away by now. He wondered if they were even bothering to think about him. To heck with them. He wouldn't think about them either.

There must be something to do. He supposed he could look around some more. The last time he'd been here, he'd been what, about five or six? He remembered going for walks, playing outside on the grass. Now nothing looked familiar.

What had his grandmother said about chickens? He didn't know anything about chickens.

He found his grandmother in the garden, picking raspberries. The dog dropped a stick at his feet, stood back wagging its tail.

Peter picked up the slimy stick, holding it with two fingers, and threw it into the bushes. The dog dashed after it, was back in two seconds, dropped the stick at his feet again.

"His name is Cousin," said his grandma. "He's a border collie. He's always herding something, sticks, or cows, or me. He'll drive you crazy, wanting to play. Sorry, I'd show you around but I've got to get these raspberries picked before they all fall on the ground."

Pete popped a couple of raspberries into his mouth. Not bad. A bit odd combined with the lingering taste of pepperoni.

"You could go to the beach if you want," his grandma said. "Do you remember where it is? It's not far; just follow the road. Cousin will show you the way."

Well, it beat standing here, shifting from foot to foot in the hot sun while his grandmother went on picking raspberries.

"Cousin, you take Pete to the beach, and take care of him, make sure he doesn't fall in," she said.

Cousin looked up at Pete's grandmother, tail wagging, then headed out of the garden. Pete followed, wondering if the dog understood English.

Pete wasn't sure he remembered the way but the dog knew. Pete followed his waving plume of a black tail down the winding road under thick dark trees, then over a wooden bridge. The creek under the bridge gurgled over golden sand. Past the bridge were what looked like old fruit trees, tangled with tall grass, weeds and thistles. Then, through a falling-down gate and down another path through more trees was the beach itself, a gold semicircle of sand set below huge granite rocks.

And that was when he had found the old rowboat, lying on the sand upside down. When he flipped it over, a pair of oars and a lifejacket were underneath it. It had seemed like a good idea at the time, take the boat out, look around. First, he sat on the sand for a while. His head was hot. He really should have worn his hat.

Who cares? he thought. Maybe if he got sunstroke, his parents would actually be sorry.

The dog had dropped a stick at his feet, and then when Pete ignored him, he began playing by himself, tossing the stick into the air, into the water, hauling it out, growling and chewing on it.

Pete had stood up, wandered around the boat, then, deliberately ignoring the lifejacket, he had put the oars in the boat and pushed it into the water. He clambered over the bow into the boat and Cousin jumped in with him, sat up on the seat in front, wagging his tail in obvious delight. And then he'd made an idiot of himself and almost drowned. Great, Pete, he thought to himself. Good way to kick off your country vacation and impress your grandmother. If she ever told his mother! Pete didn't even want to think about the long lecture on safety he would get.

—

Almost drowning yesterday had been his introduction to country life. Now, lying here on the bed, he wondered how much worse it could get.

Suddenly, his grandmother shoved open the door and stomped back into the room.

"Here," she said. "These were your dad's." She dumped a

stack of ancient comic books on his bed. "You know, this was his room."

Pete looked around the room. He knew his dad had grown up here but it had never seemed real to him. Now, in spite of himself, he was impressed when he looked at the comics — early editions of Spiderman, Batman, Sandman. His dad used to read comics? Weird. His father never talked about the farm or growing up here. The comic books were enclosed in plastic covers.

"Grandma," he said. She paused on her way out the door.

"Is there really a monster in the lake?"

"I don't know," she said. "Maybe. Some people I know have seen it. Other people have pictures of it. Okay, gotta work. I'll see you later."

After she left, he leafed through the comic books. His dad must have been collecting them. He had cared enough to put them away in plastic envelopes. Probably some of these were worth money.

Why hadn't his dad ever mentioned these? Pete lay back on the bed. He missed his parents but he didn't want to admit it. He was still too mad at them.

He spent the morning reading comic books until she called him for lunch. Lunch wasn't too bad, hamburgers and raspberries for dessert.

"So, I suppose you need a friend or two to hang out with," his grandmother said.

"I got friends," Pete mumbled.

She sat back and looked at him. Her eyes were a very

dark green. Her eyebrows were too bushy. This morning her grey hair was sticking up in short spikes. She looked strange. Pete was glad none of his friends would ever meet her.

"I can't do anything about your parents sending you here away from your friends," she said, "but I can do something to keep you from dying of boredom. C'mon, get in the truck."

Pete hadn't looked too closely at the truck before. Now when he did, he couldn't help comparing it to his dad's immaculate gold Subaru. This truck was a collection of rust and flapping fenders. The floor of the truck was covered with hay, rope, mud, dog hair and sawdust. Cousin jumped in and sat on the seat between them, looking out the window just like a person. When they pulled out of the yard, dust boiled up from holes in the floorboards. Pete perched on the edge of the seat, trying to keep his new jeans clean. He thought about his mom's brand new hybrid Prius, which no one was allowed to get into unless they washed their hands first, and a giggle came up from his throat that turned into a kind of strangled snort. He gulped and looked at his grandma to see if she had noticed.

"You like my truck, eh?" She was laughing, "Her name is Gertie. Maybe I'll let you drive her a time or two on the farm."

"Really?" Pete said.

"Well, your dad was driving a tractor when he was eight. Seems like you ought to be able to drive an old truck."

His grandma was still laughing. What a crazy old lady she was, Pete thought. He couldn't figure her out.

She seemed to read his thoughts.

"I could get a new car, maybe," she said. "But what for? I'd just be renting it from the bank. This one is old but it keeps running. Of course, it looks pretty terrible, I guess."

Pete thought about this for a while, and about his artistic musician dad, who was always worrying about protecting his hands, actually driving a tractor. While he was thinking, they arrived at their destination, a driveway winding up the mountain. It went up and up and finally they drove into a yard with a log house sitting under some giant fir trees. His grandma stopped the truck with a jerk, got out, and charged in the door of the house without knocking, with Pete sidling reluctantly behind her.

Inside, standing at the sink, a tall woman was mixing something in a bowl and a boy was sitting at the kitchen table writing in a notebook.

"Hey, Fern," his grandma said to the lady. "Hey, Jess. This here is Pete. He's here for the summer and needs a friend."

He and Jess stared at each other. Jess was tall and thin. He had wiry blond hair that stood up in corkscrew curls all over his head and bright blue eyes.

"Hey, you want to go upstairs," Jess said finally. He closed his notebook and led the way. "This is my room," he said. "This is my mom's room. She built this house with my dad. They cut all the trees down themselves."

"Nice," mumbled Pete. It seemed small and cramped to him. The log walls were grey and dusty. There was no computer, just a desk, a lot of books and a bed. Didn't any of these crazy country people have computers?

"So you're from Victoria?" said Jess.

"Yeah."

"Wow, cool, I went to the museum there once. It was amazing. Loved that woolly mammoth!"

"Oh yeah."

"Hey, you want something to eat?" Jess asked. "My mom is making chocolate chip cookies."

As they were coming back down the stairs, Pete could see that his grandma and Fern were deep in talk. They both looked serious. Fern said, "I'm so sorry, Avery, it's all my fault."

Pete's grandmother shook her head. "It's not your fault. It was my decision. But I just don't know what I'm going to do." Then she saw him coming and abruptly stopped talking. Both women looked as if they were going to start crying.

"Mom, we're starving," Jess said into the sudden silence.

"Boys," Fern said, smiling and shaking her head, "they're always hungry."

"Fresh cookies just out of the oven," she added. She put a plate on the table.

Pete picked up one of the cookies with two fingers. It was too hot but it tasted great.

After they ate, Pete's grandmother said, "Well, we'd better get back. Pete and I got work to do. That's why I got him here for the summer, keep him working. I always wanted a helper. Hey, Jess, you want to come over. Maybe you and Pete could go to the beach."

"Sure thing," Jess said.

As they were leaving, Fern gave his grandma a big hug. "Hang in there, Avery. It's my problem too. I feel responsible. We'll think of something."

They got in the truck with Jess in the middle and Pete sitting by the door, staring out the window. Jess was talking to his grandmother about something. Pete didn't talk much. It had always been that way for him. His brain could be full of thoughts and ideas but trying to get them out of his reluctant mouth, past his frozen teeth and jaws, was another matter.

When they got home, his grandma parked the truck and said, "I'm going to go upstairs and lie down for a bit. Cousin will keep you boys company."

After she disappeared into the house. Pete and Jess stood on the lawn and stared at each other. Then Pete looked at Cousin who was looking intently up at him. Cousin had very strange eyes, a kind of yellow-green colour. He stood right by Pete's leg, watching his face.

"Man, it's hot," Jess said finally. "You want to go to the beach?"

"Sure." Pete shrugged.

They turned and headed down the path, under the trees.

"So," Jess asked, "are you going to be here all summer?"

"No way," said Pete, "just a few weeks."

"Your grandmother is pretty cool, hey?"

Peter had no idea what to say to this. Was she?

"Some people think your grandma's kind of weird," Jess went on, "but my mom says she's just smarter than most people. Hey, your grandma says her dog understands English. Do you think he does?" Cousin perked up his ears and ran over to Jess, jumping up beside him.

"Hey, crazy Cousin-dog," Jess said, scratching him behind the ears. Cousin jumped up to lick his face, and Jess grabbed him around the neck and rolled over and over on the path with him, laughing. Cousin broke free, crouched on the ground, and then began racing around and around Jess, his mouth open in a happy dog grin. Then he came and sat in front of Pete.

"Go away, dog," Pete muttered.

Cousin looked at Pete, stood up and walked away, very slowly.

"Wow, he heard you," Jess said. "I think you hurt his feelings."

"He's just a dog," Pete said.

"Man, you don't know much about animals. They know stuff, they understand what you say. I used to have a dog. Boy, he even knew what I was thinking. All I had to do was think, 'walk,' and he was up and ready to go."

"So where is he, your dog?" Pete mumbled. He wasn't very interested but Jess seemed so serious.

"He got killed last winter — got in a fight with a cougar, at least we think it was a cougar. Hey, I've got an idea," Jess added. "I'll show you something cool. C'mon, follow me." Jess suddenly sprinted ahead of Pete, leaping in the air, grabbing at overhanging tree branches, trying to swing on them. Cousin followed him, leaping around Jess's feet. Jess grabbed a stick and started whirling it in the air, while Cousin followed it, leaping and barking. Pete followed more slowly.

When he finally got to the beach, Jess was still playing with the dog, throwing sticks while Cousin crashed into the water to fetch them.

"Let's go," Jess said, when Pete finally made it to the beach. He darted away, leapt onto a log and began balancing on its thin trunk.

"Follow the leader," he called. "C'mon, city boy."

Pete sighed. He wondered if Jess ever relaxed or slowed down, or did things quietly. Jess had already leapt to another log and then to the top of a rock. Pete followed him. He tried balancing on one of the logs and almost slipped and fell. After that, he climbed carefully from rock to rock, holding on. Cousin ran back and forth between them, as if trying to make sure they stayed together.

The going became rougher but now Pete was determined to keep up; he had to crawl up several of the steeper places and hang on grimly with his toes and fingers in other places.

Jess was far ahead of him now. "Hey, hurry up," Jess yelled.

By the time Pete had caught up, slipping and sliding dangerously down the sides of enormous boulders in his haste, Jess was just above him, standing on a boulder, legs spread wide, laughing,

"C'mon, city boy, let's go dive off Red Man's Point."

"What point?"

"Right over there."

Just ahead of them, a rocky point loomed up like a giant dark snout pushing into the lake water. They had to climb from hand to hand to get up the last steep pitch onto the top of the point. Cousin couldn't follow. Instead he stood at the bottom of the cliff and whined.

Then they had to scramble down again to a tiny ledge on the side of the point. Finally, Pete stood beside Jess on the ledge where they could look straight down into the black gleaming water far below — far, far below.

Jess began stripping off his clothes although he left his underwear on.

"Hey, no way," Pete said, "that water is freezing. I tried it yesterday."

"It's not that cold," Jess said. "You just have to jump in and swim hard. I've already been swimming a couple of times this year."

Slowly, Pete took off his clothes and carefully folded

them and put them on a rock. Finally he took off his new
sneakers. He kept trying to think of something to say so he
didn't have to do this. But his body and his head seemed
disconnected. Even while his head was telling him to stop,
get dressed, leave immediately, his body seemed to be getting ready to jump.

Pete was conscious of how white and skinny his legs and
arms looked next to Jess, who already had a tan.

"How far down is it?" Pete asked finally. His voice came
out thin and strangled sounding.

"Dunno," said Jess. "Far. Really far."

They both stared at the water.

"Why it is called Red Man's Point?"

"There's some old Indian pictures on it, down on the
side. You can't see them from here. One of them is this red
stick man drawing."

"Well, you gonna do it or what?" Pete asked finally. He
was thinking about the high diving board at Crystal Pool in
Victoria where he took swimming lessons. He had jumped
off it once and the water had stung when he hit it. He
thought about how icy the water had been yesterday when
he had dived in off the boat. He really didn't want to jump
in again.

"Yeah, sure," said Jess, but he didn't move. "I saw some
guys jump off here last summer."

"You ever done it before?"

"Nope, but I've thought about it. I always wanted to do it."

"You scared?"

"Yeah," Jess started to laugh. "Now that I'm up here, I'm totally freaked. But you know what, I don't think I can climb back down again. I think I got to jump. Just hang on. I got to think about it, I got to picture it in my mind. Then when it's all clear, and I can see myself doing it, then I know I can. My dad taught me that."

"Your dad?"

"He died," Jess said. "A couple of years ago. He had brain cancer." There was silence on the rock ledge.

Pete had no idea what to say. "That's awful," he managed finally.

But Jess wasn't listening to him. He was staring at the water with a faraway expression. Then quickly, he stepped to the edge of the rock, took a deep breath and jumped. He fell straight down for a long time, and then hit the water with a sound like glass shattering.

Pete held his breath, watching the pattern the splash made on the water, watching white bubbles boil to the surface. Then Jess surfaced, laughing like a crazy person.

"Wow," he yelled. "It hurts, but it's worth it. C'mon, Pete, you can do it. Fly like a bird."

Pete was cursing quietly, silently inside himself. How had he got into this mess? Why hadn't he argued with Jess, told him this was a crazy idea? Why had he just followed along like some puppet on a string, and now he was in this stupid predicament? He was too scared to jump but he didn't want to climb back down the rocks like some kind of scrawny white chicken. Except he was chicken, no question of that.

Far below, Jess was treading water, out and away from the cliff, still yelling encouragement. Pete closed his eyes and took a deep breath. The sun was hot on his skin. He should be wearing a hat. If his mother were here, she'd tell him to get down off this crazy rock, go put his clothes back on, put on a hat and sunscreen, and be sensible.

He stepped to the edge of the rock, took a deep breath. He tried to do what Jess had said: picture himself hurtling through the air. But all it did was send a new thrill of sick fear through his gut. He felt like he was going to throw up.

"Jump straight down," Jess yelled. "Don't go sideways or it'll really hurt."

He was going to have to do it. There was no other way down off this stupid cliff and out of this mess. He took another deep breath and jumped. He seemed to fall for a long time — then suddenly the green, freezing water was crashing around him and he was inside it, going down and down, into its black depths, down farther than he wanted to go. Involuntarily, he opened his eyes and found himself looking at something he couldn't quite understand, something that looked like a long tentacle or rope extending upwards from the blackness towards him. In terror, he twisted away and kicked furiously to push his way back to the surface. He came out of the water gasping and choking, coughing and gagging.

Jess was beside him, laughing. "Hey man, we did it. That's so cool!"

But Pete was still gasping in terror. "There's something down there, something spooky, let's get out of here."

"What?" Jess yelled. "What did you see?"

But Pete was paddling furiously for the rocks, expecting that slimy tentacle to wrap around his leg at any moment. "Hurry," he yelled at Jess. "Get away from there."

On the rocks, Cousin was barking furiously. Pete finally reached the shore and hauled himself out of the water with Jess right behind him.

They lay side by side on the warm rocks, catching their breath.

"Oh, man," Jess said, sitting up. "That was so amazing. Wow, that water was so cold. I always wanted to do that. So what did you see down there that had you so freaked out? Man, I thought a shark was after you."

"I dunno," Pete said. Now that they were back on dry land, he was beginning to think he had really made a fool of himself, freaking out like that. "It was kind of long and streaky, like an octopus, or something."

"Oh that's just weeds," Jess said. "They're like seaweed, they grow up out of the lake bottom."

"Maybe," Pete agreed. "Maybe that's all it was."

"Hey, you're okay for a city boy," Jess said. "Man, that was a crazy thing to do, hey?" Jess was laughing again. "Just wait until I tell my friend Bird. Her real name is Robin so I call her Bird. She'll be so jealous. We're gonna have some good times this summer, you just wait."

Chapter Three

—

"Grandma?" Pete said the next morning over breakfast. His grandmother had made pancakes and Pete was slathering them with butter and jam. "Why is Cousin so weird?"

"Weird, my wonderful dog weird? What do you mean?" She looked to where Cousin was lying on the floor. He paid no attention to them; he was sleeping on his back with his paws folded together. He looked like a big furry baby.

"He seems to understand stuff."

"What kind of stuff?"

"Like what you say."

"Well, of course he does."

Pete stared at her.

"Animals aren't stupid, you know. Of course they understand what you say."

"All kinds of animals?"

"Yes, of course," she said.

"You talk to animals?"

"All the time. You should try it."

"Uh, no thanks." He looked down, embarrassed.

"Listen, Pete. I wanted to ask you about something. I have to go into town. I'd take you but you'd be bored stiff. I have to go to the bank, do bank things. You're old enough to stay on your own, right? Or there's a bike out in the woodshed, if you want to go see Jess. I got it fixed when I heard you were coming."

"Yeah, all right." Pete's mom had never left him home alone once in his life. She seemed to think he might burn the house down or be murdered by burglars if he wasn't watched all the time. And now he would have a whole farm to himself.

"I'll be home for lunch," she said. "If you get hungry, there's raspberries in the garden and chocolate ice cream in the fridge. Oh, and if you remember, you could give the compost to the chickens. See you, sweetheart."

He stared after her. Cousin was also awake and watched her go out the door. Then he turned his strange yellow eyes on Pete.

"Cousin, go get a ball," Pete said. Cousin ignored him, rolled over on his back, put his paws in the air and appeared to go back to sleep.

Okay, thought Pete, so much for talking animals. Maybe his grandma really was crazy, the locking-up kind of crazy. He finished his pancakes, took his plate to the sink, and then hesitated. At his house, dishes were washed the minute they got dirty. His mother would whisk his plate out from under his nose the minute he finished eating. The plate would be scrubbed and put away before Pete got up from the table. But his grandma's plate, the mixing bowl for the pancakes, even the frying pan were stacked on the counter at the edge of the sink. Pete put his plate on top of his grandma's. He stared out the window at the sunny yard.

The house felt very big and lonely without his grandmother there. It was also very quiet. He hadn't yet been upstairs where his grandmother slept. He crept up the stairs, which creaked under his feet. The door to her room was closed. Hesitantly, he put out one finger and pushed it open. He stood in the open doorway staring at the room. The bed wasn't made, but the sun poured in from the glass doors at the other end of the room, which opened onto a small deck. Two of the walls were covered with bookshelves and stacks of books.

There was a desk in the corner with a notebook computer that was almost buried under books and papers. So there was a computer. Why hadn't his grandmother mentioned it? He stepped softly across the bare floorboards to the computer. He reached out, touched the computer keys and the screen came to life. "Log in," it said. Halfheartedly, Pete tried a few combinations of words and numbers but nothing worked. He began turning over the papers and books. He didn't recognize any of the titles. Then he looked at the shelf over the desk. Several of the books there had his grandma's name on the spine. He opened one. Poetry. He had never liked poetry. He tried to read one or two of the poems anyway. One poem was about the lake, another one about walking in the forest with a dog. They were pretty, he thought. How did someone learn to write poetry, anyway? Maybe he could ask his grandmother sometime.

He looked around the rest of the room. There were his school pictures, a picture of his dad, and another one of his mom and dad together. There were framed photographs on the wall. One was of his grandmother receiving some kind of award.

Suddenly, Pete had the distinct impression that someone was watching him. He whirled around; it was only Cousin.

"You scared me, dog," he said. But Cousin just stared at him, then went to the top of the stairs and came back again. He came into the room, sniffed anxiously at the rumpled bed, and then trotted back to the stairs. Then he returned to the room and stared at Pete some more. There was something in his look that made Pete feel guilty.

"Okay," he said, "okay, I'm leaving." Cousin wagged his

tail and ran back down the stairs without waiting for Pete.

Pete followed him. Maybe there was something to do outside. He hadn't had time to explore the whole farm yet. He knew only that there were a couple of cows, some chickens, and the big garden. He went out the back steps and Cousin bounded ahead of him.

It was already hot, even so early in the morning. Maybe Jess would come by and want to go swimming again. His back had stung all yesterday afternoon from hitting the water so hard but it was a good pain. He was proud of it.

He stood still in the yard. It was very quiet; none of the noises he was used to. No cars, no faraway sirens, no planes overhead, no phones ringing. A rooster crowed. Right, he was supposed to feed the chickens. He went back in the house, found the compost bucket on the sink, and carried it outside and over to the pen where a bunch of brown chickens were scratching in the dust. He dumped out a pile of apple and potato peels, and mouldy raspberries. It looked totally gross but the chickens didn't seem to mind. They went right to work scratching and pecking at the food.

He watched them for a while. He didn't know anything about any of this: animals, farming. He missed his computer. He missed being immersed in a game, shooting bad guys, moving fast, not having to think. He was determined not to think about his parents, but now, when he remembered his mom's voice when she said, so carefully, "Your dad and I will be living in separate houses," he felt sick. She had gone on talking after that but he hadn't listened. He hadn't wanted to listen to her ever again. Everything had been a blur until he found himself here.

He left the chickens and wandered down to the garden, past the raspberry bushes, stopping to pick a few. The garden was full of flowers and plants he didn't recognize. His mom grew a flower garden every year. She was always trying to get him to come and help but he wasn't interested.

The raspberries were sweet in his mouth. He picked a few more, then turned to wander back up to the house. A car coming along the highway, slowed, and turned into his grandmother's driveway. Pete wasn't sure what to do. The car, a black Mercedes SUV, pulled into the yard and stopped. A man opened the door, got out and stood looking around. He was wearing a suit and tie. His face was red and sweaty and his belly stuck out in front of him. Pete walked towards him.

"Hi kid," he said cheerfully. "Where's the lady who lives here?"

Cousin was barking and growling at the man.

"Hey kid," the man said, "call off your dog."

Pete didn't know what to say. He opened his mouth but no words came out. Finally he said, "Cousin, come here. Be quiet."

Cousin ignored him. Pete had to raise his voice over the barking.

"She went to town. She'll be home soon."

"Well, I'll just look around on my own then," the man said. "Keep that dog under control, will you?"

The man went to his car and took out a BlackBerry, a camera, and a measuring tape. Pete stood still, with Cousin at his feet. Cousin had stopped barking and now he was looking up at Pete. Pete wondered if he should do anything. The man disappeared around the corner of the house, but Pete could hear him whistling.

He followed the man to the back door of the house. He had pulled a camera out of his pocket and was taking pictures. Every once in a while he stopped to write something on his BlackBerry.

Pete watched him.

He took some more pictures of the house, then wandered around the yard, humming to himself.

Finally, he came back to Pete.

"Here's my card," he said. "Tell the lady I was here, will you? She'll know what it's about."

Pete didn't say anything. He looked at the card in his hand. Ed Paterson, it read. Real Estate. Why was a real estate agent looking at his grandmother's house? Was she selling the farm?

Once the SUV pulled out of the yard, Pete was left alone in the silence again. Cousin picked up a stick and dropped it at his feet.

Pete sighed. "You never give up, dog, do you?"

Moodily, he wandered over to the barnyard fence, then

slipped between the rails. There was a barn and a couple of brown and white cows grazing, heads down, out in the middle of the field. He stopped for a moment. Did cows chase people? But they didn't seem even remotely interested in him, so he kept going.

The barn was made of huge round logs. Pete opened the door and peered inside. It was dusty and smelled funny. He spotted a ladder on the side of the barn, climbed up and found himself in a hayloft where a few bales of hay were stacked against one wall. There was a big square hole in the front of the loft and he sat down on the floor with his legs dangling over the wall.

Suddenly he heard a scrambling sound and Cousin came from somewhere back of the hayloft and sat down beside him.

"Hey, how did you get up here?"

Pete reached out his hand and touched the soft fur behind Cousin's ears and Cousin swiped at his face with a pink tongue. Actually, Pete had always wanted a dog of his own, but his mother said dogs were a nuisance. They left hair on the carpet, they had to be walked, they smelled. She had offered to get him a hamster but that didn't seem like much of a substitute for a dog.

Cousin went on sitting beside Pete and staring out over the drowsy, silent field. His ears twitched and so did his nose.

Pete tried to think if he had ever been in this barn before.

He didn't remember much about the farm but he did remember that he had really loved coming here with his parents when he was little. But then, for some reason, they never came again. Instead, his grandmother came to stay with them in Victoria. When she came, she made a fuss over him, took him shopping, took him to a movie or to Murchie's for hot chocolate. But then when he was about nine, she stopped coming. His mother said something about his grandmother not being able to travel, but he hadn't paid attention. What had happened? Why didn't he know?

And why didn't his dad ever talk about this place? He had grown up here. Maybe he had sat in this same place looking out over this field. Had it always felt like this in the summer, peaceful and still?

The emerald grass glowed softly under the beating of the sun. There was a line of golden-green leafy trees at the edge of the field and beyond that, darker forest and mountains. The air was silent. The farm felt both mysterious and familiar, as if he had always been here.

And when was the last time he had spent time alone? He spent a lot of time in Victoria alone in his room but that didn't count. In his room he had a television, a computer, and a stereo. When he went outside to go to school or to the mall, he wore headphones and listened to music.

He heard a distant shrill cry and looked up. There were a couple of large birds circling in the sky. He didn't know but he guessed they might be hawks. Cousin watched them for a moment and then relaxed again. But his nose went on wrinkling, sniffing, and testing the air. His ears swivelled with every sound. He seemed to notice everything.

The problem with sitting here was that Pete had nothing to distract himself with, to keep him from thinking about the problem of his parents. What was going to happen when he went home? Would he have to go back and forth between his parents, packing his things in his backpack? Or would he stay with his mother and see his dad less and less, like most of the kids he knew whose parents had split up? He knew his parents didn't get along that well because they hardly ever talked to each other. They were always so busy. But they never fought either, so how was he to know if they were getting along or not?

No matter how much he tried not to think about them, it still made him hurt inside, as if his guts were twisting themselves into knots. Maybe he'd stay here forever. That would fix them. They probably wouldn't even miss him.

From far away, Pete heard another vehicle coming along the highway. Then it turned into the yard. Cousin took off like a small black and white bullet. Pete scrambled down the ladder and then through the fence. To his relief, it was his grandmother.

His grandma waved, pulled two bags of groceries out of the truck, and then trudged into the house with Pete right behind her. Inside, she pulled groceries out of the bags, turned the electric kettle on, broke open a bag of chips and poured them into a bowl, then plunked a can of Coke on the table in front of Pete. After she had made a pot of tea, she poured herself a cup and sat down with a heavy sigh. His mother never allowed him to drink Coke. Whenever he asked for a Coke, she always made the same speech, about how Coke was bad for your teeth, how it was just expensive, coloured, sugary water, how aluminum cans were bad for the environment and how the Coca-Cola company exploited poor people around the world.

"Grandma, some guy was here," Pete said and handed her the card. She stared at it for a moment and then threw it on the table.

This morning she was wearing a white blouse instead of a sweatshirt, and a flowered skirt. She even had on a bit of makeup. For an old lady, she was kind of pretty. He suddenly realized how much she looked like his dad. And since everyone said Pete looked like his dad, he must look like his grandmother.

As if reading his mind, she said, "You look so much like your dad." She smiled. "You know, it is so great having you here but it's pretty scary for me."

"What!"

"What if you get bored, what if you run away, what if you hurt yourself? Fern told me about you and Jess jumping off the point yesterday. That isn't the smartest thing I've ever heard of. Pete, we've got to figure some stuff out so this visit is good for both of us."

He squirmed in his chair. Jess shouldn't have told.

"By the way," she said finally, "what's with your parents?"

Now it was his turn to stare.

"Pete, I've missed you a lot but didn't your parents realize that sending you to spend the summer with an old lady you hardly know, on a farm in the country, is probably going to bore you to death?"

This was too close to his own thoughts for comfort.

"You're not boring," he mumbled. She stared at him and raised her eyebrows.

"They're splitting up," he said at last. "Dad is going to Europe for the summer on tour, and Mom has to go to Africa to teach. I was supposed to stay with my friend Oren, but then his father got a transfer. Dad is getting his own place in the fall." He bowed his head, feeling his cheeks turning red. He hated even saying the words. "They didn't have anywhere else to leave me."

His grandmother nodded. "I knew it was something like that. Your mom and dad didn't tell me much. Your mom phoned and said they were a bit desperate and wouldn't it be great for us to spend some time together. She told me your dad was thinking of getting his own place and they thought you were really upset. So I guess they sent you here, thinking it might be good for us to both be miserable together. Your dad used to tell me things about his life but now he's too busy. I haven't really talked to him for years and I missed seeing you. But they were always so busy when

I phoned or wanted to come down. They must be pretty unhappy, both of them."

"I don't know," Pete said. It hadn't occurred to him to wonder how they were feeling. Besides, he thought, he was still too mad to care. If they were miserable, it was their own fault.

"Pete, when your mom phoned to ask if you could come, she said she would send a letter with you telling me all about your diet, so I can figure out how to feed you properly. I just bought food for you I figured I would have liked when I was a kid. What do you like to eat?"

"Whatever," he shrugged. He grinned. "I never get this at home." He lifted the can of Coke and took a big swallow. His grandmother laughed.

"Do you like computers?"

"Well, yeah."

"You know how to find stuff on the Internet, how to do email and all that, right? Did you check out my computer? Pretty neat, eh?"

"Yeah." He felt his cheeks redden. How had she guessed?

"Well, you can use it all you want. But I don't have any games or anything like that."

"That's okay," he said. "You can download them. I can show you how."

"Yeah? That'd be great. Maybe you can show me how to play them. So where's this letter of your mother's?"

He stood up, went to his room, pulled out the black

nylon case with the letter. The case was full of aspirin, vitamins, an asthma inhaler, and a kit he could use if he were
stung by a bee and couldn't breathe. He put it in front of his
grandmother and slumped back into his chair. Now she
was going to think he was a total nerd. She looked carefully through the case, and read the letter. She nodded her
head.

"Okay," she said. "I read it. Now what say we put this case
of stuff up here on the shelf so it will be handy if we need
it. And let's make a deal. I'll make the food I like, and if you
don't like it, you tell me and I'll make you something else.
Deal?"

He nodded.

"So, how did you and Jess get along?"

"Okay."

She nodded again. Then she laughed. "He's a good kid.
His mom Fern is my best friend. Did he tell you his dad
died?"

Pete nodded. He said cautiously, "He sure talks a lot."

"Yep, he loves talking. Not like you, that's for sure. You
know, Pete, sometimes talking is just a lot of noise and
sometimes it's useful. The trick is to tell the difference. Jess
usually has something interesting to say."

Peter thought about this. It made a lot of sense.

"So did your dad tell you lots of stories about the farm
and the stuff he did when he was a kid?"

"No. He never talks about the farm. Was that really his
room?"

"Sure was." Her face suddenly looked sad. "Pete, your dad and I had a pretty hard time when he was growing up. I left his father when he was very small. We lived here with my father, your great-grandpa. But my dad was a grumpy old coot. And we were always poor. Your dad was such a gifted musician and there weren't any really good music teachers around here. I tried hard to get him what he needed but I think he felt trapped. He left for the city as soon as he got out of high school, and he hates coming back here. He's been after me for years to sell the farm and move to the city."

"So who was that guy this morning?"

"Oh, he's a real estate dealer. He's just doing an assessment to see what the place is worth. I asked him to do it. But he's afraid of dogs, and Cousin hates him."

"Are you going to sell the farm?"

Her face changed. It was like a shadow passing over the sun. "I don't know, Pete. I haven't made any decisions yet. I don't know what I'm going to do."

"Grandma?"

"Yes, Pete."

Pete paused. What did he really want to say? He just wanted to make her smile again.

"How did my dad learn to drive a tractor?"

"Now that's a good story." She laughed and settled back in her chair. "You know, I've got so many stories to tell you, Pete. Maybe this will turn out to be a good summer after all. Your dad actually wasn't much interested in farming or

farm work and he sure wasn't interested in driving the tractor. But there were only the three of us to do all the work,
so your dad had to learn to drive the tractor at haying time.
Your great-grandpa was a terrible teacher. He used to just
yell at your dad until he figured out what was wrong. One
day he told your poor dad to get up on the tractor, showed
him the gears and the brake and yelled at him, 'Now, get
going.' Your dad was so scared he started the tractor and
drove backwards over his grandpa's foot. Then when his
grandpa started yelling, he drove forward and went right
over his foot again."

Grandma laughed. "He wasn't hurt because the ground
was soft. Your dad actually became a pretty good driver
after that. His grandpa limped around for a week com-
plaining his foot was broken but when I tried to get him to
go to a doctor, he just said doctors were fools."

"Wow!" Pete said. He tried to picture his father on a tractor but he couldn't. His mom always complained that his
father wouldn't do any work around the house.

"Grandma?" Pete said. "Can you tell me another story
about my dad?"

"Sure." She thought for a moment. "Your dad loved to
collect things — comic books, Lego, hats, and even stuffed
toys. When he was five or six, he had this enormous collection of toy guns. He loved to dress up and play that he was
Superman or some other comic book hero. I used to wonder if he was ever going to live in the real world or just a
make-believe one."

"Wow, really?" Pete sat back. He hadn't known any of this stuff.

"What else?"

"Pete, I promise I will tell you lots of stories but not right now. Let's have some lunch and then I've got to go pick those darn raspberries again. Maybe I'll make a pie."

Chapter Four

—

Pete was lying on his bed reading comics. It was evening. Cousin was lying beside him on the bed, also on his back, with his paws folded together. He looked very silly.

Pete had spent the morning downloading games on the computer and helping his grandmother with the farm chores. He had met both the cows and the flock of multi-coloured chickens. His grandmother had taken him all over the farm, showing him the places where his dad used to play. In the afternoon, they went to the beach and along the rocks to a cave made by two giant slabs of rock that had slid against one another.

"I love this cave," his grandmother said. "I used to hide

here from my dad to get out of working when I was a kid. It's a great place for a hideout. You and Jess could go camping here sometime."

Then they went back to the beach and his grandmother pulled two folding chairs and an umbrella out from under the canoe. His grandmother said she didn't swim anymore; it made her bones ache. Instead, she sat in the chair with a book. Pete swam and dived off the rocks and then when he was cold, he sat on the sand beside her. She had brought chips and lemonade and they finished all of it.

"Hey, want to see something neat?" she asked, when they were done.

They took the rowboat over to Red Man's Point with Pete rowing carefully and his grandma and Cousin sitting on the seat side by side. When they got to the dark snout of rock that he and Jess had climbed, she showed him the Indian pictographs on the rock. The pictographs showed a circle with lines coming out of it, a red figure, and some other smaller figures that were so faded they were hard to see.

That night, after supper, she showed him a book about the other Indian pictographs that were found all around the lake. They talked about maybe taking the rowboat out one day to look for some of them.

"But what were the pictographs for?" Pete asked. "What did they mean?"

"I asked a First Nations friend of mine that," his grandma said. "He said they were special places where people went when they wanted to learn something."

"So there were native peoples here before there were white people?"

"They lived at the south end of the lake, and they came here to fish and to camp. There's a bunch of stuff on the Internet about it, if you want to look."

"So when did white people get here? Where did we come from?"

"Well, your great-great grandfather, who was my grand-father, came here from Ontario, but his father came from Scotland. And his wife came from France. They met in a logging camp in northern Ontario. Your great-great-grand-mother was cooking for a whole camp full of men when she was only eighteen."

Pete was silent, thinking about this.

"Grandma," he said finally.

"Yes, sugar." Whenever she looked at him, she always had this big smile on her face. She seemed to approve of what-ever he did. Even this afternoon, she had complimented him on his swimming ability, and on his strength as a rower.

"It's sure different here. From home, I mean."

"Peter, it just makes me so happy that you're here. Whatever your poor parents are dealing with, this visit is a good thing for me, that's for sure."

The next morning, Jess flew into the yard on his bike, skid-ded to a halt, and flopped down, puffing, beside Pete, who was lying on his back on the grass with Cousin beside him. Cousin rolled on his back so Jess could scratch his belly. Pete had a handful of gingersnap cookies and he gave two to Jess and one to Cousin. Then they all stared at the sky together. It was a deep clear blue with little plops of cloud in only a few places.

"There was a really weird guy here a few days ago," Pete said finally.

"The guy who wants to buy your grandma's farm or something. Yeah, I heard."

Pete looked at him in surprise.

"My mom and your grandmother are always talking about stuff," Jess said.

Pete kept staring. "Hey, it's a small place," Jess said. "My mom always says, if you get up here in the morning and sneeze, all day people will ask about your cold. So, what's the story? Is she selling the farm?"

"I don't know. I asked but she said she hadn't decided."

"Wow," Jess said. "That would be a big drag. She's been here forever."

"My dad grew up here. It used to belong to my grandfather."

"Wow, that's cool. What else you been up to?"

"My grandma has a computer. I've downloaded some games and stuff."

"Hey," Jess interrupted. "You gotta meet my friend Bird. She knows all about computers too. She really wants to meet you. I told her I'd bring you over. We can go on our bikes. It's just up the road."

Bird lived in a big white house with wide screened verandas. It was up a broad winding driveway lined with trees. There were horses grazing in the fields that were surrounded by white fences.

"Bird's dad is a doctor," Jess said. "Her mom does something with computers."

Bird saw them from the deck and waved as they came up the driveway. She was standing in the driveway when they got off their bikes. She was taller than Pete and had long brownish-red hair in braids, brown eyes, and lots of freckles. She was wearing blue jeans and a white sweater.

She looked at Pete through narrowed eyes and he felt his mouth go dry.

Jess said, "This is Pete. He's from the big city."

Pete frowned. Jess made it sound as though Pete had some kind of mental illness.

Bird was still looking at him. "I feel like I've seen you somewhere before?"

"No, I don't think so." Pete was having a hard time saying anything. He was afraid of girls. Especially smart girls who looked at him like he was some kind of bug.

"Oh, I know. I've seen your picture. Maybe it was in one of your grandma's books."

"You've read her books?"

"I tried. She's supposed to be a wonderful poet. My father says she is an undiscovered treasure."

"Oh."

"So how come we've never seen you here before?"

Pete turned red. Suddenly all he wanted to do was turn around and go home. Words clogged in his throat and stuck there.

"C'mon," Bird said, "let's go get a snack and you can tell me about it."

Jess and Bird went into Bird's big fancy house with Pete trailing behind. The kitchen was bright with sunlight — there were big glass doors that opened onto a wide deck. Soon Jess and Bird were heating up frozen pizza, laughing together and talking about people Pete didn't know. Pete went out on the deck and sat at the glass table and stared at the view. From here, he could see out over the whole valley, over the lake and the mountains. Big white clouds were piled on the mountains like clumps of whipped cream. Jess and Bird were still talking and ignoring him. His feet felt too big and he shoved them under the table, then his hands felt too big and he pushed them into the pockets of his jeans.

Jess and Bird set the pizzas on the table along with glasses of iced tea.

"So what's your story, Pete?" Bird said. "What do you do in Victoria?"

"Oh, just hang out and stuff."

"So what are you doing here for the summer?"

Pete shrugged. "My parents needed a babysitter."

It hadn't come out right. It wasn't what he had meant to

say at all. His face burned. He stared at his uneaten pizza.

They were both silent now, staring at him.

"Something wrong with your pizza?" Bird said.

"No, it's fine." Pete was feeling more and more uncomfortable. He kept thinking of things to say but none of them would come out of his mouth. As soon as he thought of saying them, they sounded stupid in his head. He felt his face turning red. He took too big a bite of the pizza and almost choked and then he had to swallow a big gulp of iced tea to wash it down.

Bird narrowed her eyes. "Your grandmother is one of the coolest people around here. And that farm is so beautiful. You're so lucky you get to spend some time there."

"Yeah, it's okay."

Bird and Jess looked at each other.

"So, Pete, Jess says you're some kind of computer dude."

"What? Me? No, I play a few games, that's about it." Pete shot an angry look at Jess. The guy had the biggest mouth. They finished their pizza.

"So why don't you show us how smart you are. C'mon," Bird said and led them upstairs to her room. She had a brand new laptop computer sitting on her desk.

"First, let's play some games," Bird said, moving towards the desk. "Do you know StarQuest? I am, like, the StarQuest queen."

Later, as Pete bicycled home through the dusk, his head was buzzing. They had spent the afternoon playing computer games and then Bird had showed them all over her farm. It was a beautiful place. There was a big red barn, a pair of horses grazing behind a white rail fence, a big garden, and fruit trees. Everything was immaculately cared for. It was very different from his grandmother's farm, where everything was kind of messy and falling apart.

Bird had asked him all kinds of nosy questions about his grandmother, most of which he couldn't answer.

He was beginning to realize he had more questions than answers about his family. When had his grandmother stopped coming to visit? Why weren't his parents proud of her if she was such a great writer? Why hadn't his father told him stories about growing up on the farm?

Something black zipped by his head and he ducked but then he realized it was probably only a bat. It was getting dark, not the greatest time to be bicycling down a deserted country road. What if he met a bear or some other wild animal? He didn't know much about bears. Were you supposed to keep going towards them or turn around and ride away?

A flash of light flickered behind the mountains across the lake, followed by a roll of thunder. He came to a steep hill, and began to struggle up it, puffing, bent over the handlebars. Something rustled and cracked in the brush above the highway, and he managed to put on a sudden burst of speed. More lightning crackled across the sky, closer this time. The thunder was definitely getting louder. He pedalled furiously. He could see some lights in the distance and he hoped desperately it was his grandmother's house. He didn't know quite where he was any more. Finally, he made it to the top of the big hill and now he was speeding down the other side — and then something black rushed across the road in front of him just as another bolt of lightning smacked onto the mountainside above him. This time the thunder was deafening. All he could do was keep going even though it felt like his hair was standing up on his head from fear. In another few minutes, he pedalled into his grandmother's yard, slammed the bike into the woodshed and raced into the house. His grandmother was sitting at the table reading.

"Pete, I was just getting ready to come and look for you," she said. He fell into a chair.

"Man, that was scary. Lightning! And something ran across the road."

"It was probably a deer."

Just then there was another clap of thunder and the lights went out.

"Sit still," his grandma said. "It happens all the time, every storm. I've got candles." She struck a match, lit some candles, and then put them in the middle of table.

"Are you hungry, Pete?"

"I had pizza at Bird's."

"Bird — now there's a wonderful young woman. I hope you will be good friends with her and Jess, then you'll have fun here. Maybe you'll even come back someday."

Pete was silent. What did he want to say? "It's just . . . Grandma . . . ?"

"Yes, Pete?"

"How come you don't visit anymore? You used to come around all the time when I was little."

"Yes, I did," she said. "You were the greatest kid. I used to have so much fun hanging out with you."

"So, what happened?"

His grandmother sighed. "It's complicated," she said. "Your father and I had a fight, a bad one. Your father and I both have terrible tempers and we said some foolish things." She paused. Pete waited. She looked at him.

"You don't need to hear about this, Pete. It's all old stuff."

Pete didn't say anything. He just kept looking at her.

She sighed. "After my dad died and left me this farm, your father wanted me to sell and move to the coast. He said I would never get known as a poet buried off here in the country. He was right, of course. Plus living here meant I couldn't get a job and make some money. And of course, poetry doesn't make any money and neither does farming. I was always so broke and it costs money to travel, and your mom and dad were always so busy. I couldn't ask them for help. So I put it off. I realize now I should have just come anyway. I missed you so much. Your dad kept after me to sell the farm, move to the city, and he kept making me mad all over again. I didn't want to do that. I grew up here. I love this place, Pete. It's my home."

Pete nodded. They were both silent for a bit.

"It was my fault, really," his grandma said. Her face twisted as if she might cry. "I should have tried harder. I should have called. Now I don't know what to do. Your father and I still love each other. I just don't know what to say to him anymore. I guess I'm just scared to try again. I can't stand it when he gets so mad at me."

Pete was silent, thinking all this over. "What if I phone my dad when he gets back from the tour and ask him to come and see you?"

"Oh, he's so busy," she said. "Just leave it, Pete. It isn't your problem."

He wanted to say, yes, it is my problem, but while he was hesitating she said, "Hey, listen to that thunder. Let's go outside and watch the lightning! I hope you don't mind storms. We get them a lot in the summer."

"No way. I'm not going out there."

"Oh come on. It's beautiful."

Reluctantly, he followed her out into the now pitch-black yard. Lightning was forking and branching across the sky in amazing long arcs of blazing light. Huge crashing thumps of thunder followed every flash. Pete had never seen anything like it.

"It'll start to rain soon," his grandmother shouted. "That will put out any fires that the lightning starts."

Pete stood staring up at the violent, flashing, fiery sky. It was scary but exciting. Cousin came and crowded up against his legs. He stood there until the first drops of rain hit his upturned face. Then suddenly the rain turned into a solid wall of water. He yelped and sprinted for the house, his grandmother behind him. She was laughing, shaking the rain out of her hair.

"Oh, that was so great. I am so glad you were here to see it, too. C'mon, we'll light a fire in the fireplace, make some hot chocolate and toast marshmallows over the fire."

Soon they were sitting on cushions in front of the glowing fire.

"Grandma," Pete said, "who made this farm?"

"My grandfather, your great-great grandfather, bought the farm for taxes, after the original settler, Pierre Longine, died." She hesitated.

"What happened to him?" Pete asked.

"It's a very strange story and no one understands what happened. Your great-great-grandfather and Pierre were friends. Just before he died, Pierre told my grandfather a really strange story. My grandfather said they stayed up late one night drinking whiskey, and Pierre got talking because he was drunk. He told my grandpa he had a stash of gold coins that he had won playing poker with the miners across the lake, and he had hidden them. But he thought some of the miners wanted to steal the gold. He said he had made a map of where he had hidden it, and he was going to give it to my grandpa in case anything happened to him. He said my grandpa was the only person he could trust. My grandpa said he thought Pierre had gone crazy from being alone too much."

She paused, staring into the fire. "Pierre was a young man when he came here, just eighteen or nineteen. But people grew up fast then. He worked so hard, Grandpa said. He cut down trees and built a barn and a house, he made fences out of split cedar rails, and those same fences are still standing out there today. He built a chicken house and a log woodshed. I don't know how he did it all. He had a sawmill and he made all his own lumber from the trees he cleared off the pasture. He had goats, chickens, a team of horses, a milk cow, all kinds of animals. Grandpa said he used to go prospecting too, in his spare time, looking for more gold I guess. In those days, everyone thought they could strike it rich mining."

Pete thought about that, thought about how it might be to be young and in a new country, on land where no one else had lived except Indians. He sighed.

"That must have been so cool," he said. "I never really thought about it before. When they talked about history in school, it just sounded boring."

"I like to think about it too," his grandmother said.

"How did he die?" Pete asked.

"Well, that's the mysterious part. He and Grandpa stayed up late. I think they had a bit too much whiskey to drink. My grandpa always liked a drop of whiskey. In the morning, Grandpa left. He came back a few days later, but there was no sign of Pierre. The animals hadn't been fed. Grandpa got some other people to help look but no one found anything. After Grandpa bought the farm, he kept on looking for Pierre's body and his stash of gold. When I was a kid, I looked for it too but I never found it. We sure could have used the money. I always felt guilt that I couldn't buy your dad what he wanted. He deserved better."

"Wow, do you think the gold is still hidden somewhere? Maybe I could find it."

"We looked everywhere. Oh, I shouldn't have told you about it, Pete. Maybe I am just being a foolish, romantic old woman and your father is right, I should sell this place, buy myself a nice condo in the city somewhere, and forget the whole thing. It would sure be a relief not to worry about money anymore."

In the light from the fireplace, she suddenly looked very old. Black shadows covered the lower part of her face. Her grey hair was straggling into her eyes. She did look kind of witch-like.

"I'm sorry, Pete," she said. "I'm wrong to tell you my troubles. They're not your problem, or Jess or Bird's problem either. I don't want you to worry about me. There's this resort company that wants to buy the farm. That's why I got Ed to come and do an assessment. They've been phoning, and bugging me. I guess they're not bad people but they make me mad. Still, they have a lot of money. Maybe it doesn't matter what I want. Who cares if this farm gets turned into condos, or cottages or a golf course."

Pete didn't know what to say. His head was still busy with pictures from the story she had told.

"Pete, my troubles are not your responsibility. Look,

sweetie, I'm going to bed. You can stay up by the fire for a while if you want." She looked like she was going to cry. She stood up awkwardly, then swayed by the chair. Pete leapt up.

"Grandma!"

"I'm okay, honey, just a bit dizzy. I'll see you in the morning." She disappeared up the stairs with Cousin at her heels. Pete sat and stared at the fire for along time, his head full of questions.

Chapter Five

—

"So where would you hide gold if you didn't want anyone to find it?" Bird said. "We should try and think like Pierre. We have to imagine the farm the way it was eighty years ago. Maybe the lake was lower or higher. Maybe there were caves in the rocks."

"We're in a cave in the rocks," Jess said. Pete looked around. They were sitting in the cave Pete's grandmother had shown him. Outside the sun was beating down on the lake surface. Light jumped and bounced off the small waves, making crazy jigsaw patterns on the cave walls. They were all in bathing suits but they hadn't gone swimming.

"Other caves, I mean," Bird said, a note of impatience in her voice. "If there's this cave, there might be more. We should look along the shore line."

"But wouldn't everyone else have already looked there?" Pete asked.

Bird glared at him. "I don't hear you coming up with better ideas."

Pete sighed. No matter what he said, it seemed to irritate Bird. She was always looking at him as if he didn't have a brain in his head. But no matter what Jess said, even if Pete thought it was kind of dopey, Bird laughed like it was brilliant.

"You said we should think like Pierre," Pete argued. "So why would he hide his gold in a cave in the rocks? That's the first place people would look."

"It might be hidden somewhere else," Jess said. "Maybe a tunnel or something. I'll bet the entrance is covered over with something, or maybe there's a secret door, or a hidden entrance."

"Didn't Pierre build your grandma's house?" Bird said. "Maybe there's a secret compartment in that house."

"Grandma said he built the house and a barn and a chicken shed but her father tore them down. She said she looked through everything when she was a kid but no luck."

"We have to think harder," Bird said, wrinkling her forehead. "If everyone has already looked everywhere for this stupid gold, then there is only one logical answer — it's in a place no one has thought of yet."

"Hey, that's brilliant," Jess said.

I already thought of that, Pete said to himself. But it didn't matter. Jess and Bird were a team and he was on the outside looking in.

"Or it's gone because someone else found it," Pete said. Bird gave him a look as if he had just said something really lame.

"I say we start with the house," Bird decided. "We should go over the house from top to bottom. I think we also have to talk to Avery, see what she knows, what she remembers. But we have to be careful not to upset her. She's already got a lot to deal with."

It made Pete uncomfortable to hear Bird refer to his grandmother by her name. She was *his* grandmother. Bird seemed to think she knew his own grandmother better than he did.

"I talked to her about selling the farm," he said uncomfortably.

"What did she say?" Bird looked at him like he was bug.

"Well, actually, she got upset. She doesn't want to sell the farm but some resort people are bugging her and phoning her all the time. She said I shouldn't worry about it. After that, she started to cry."

"You must have said something wrong."

"No, I didn't."

"I'm going to talk to her about this story of the gold," Bird said decisively. "We need to know where she looked and see if there is anything she might have missed. You probably got some of the details wrong."

Once again, words were choking and tangling in Pete's throat. He felt as if he couldn't breathe, as if all the words boiling inside him were cutting off the air. Bird thought she was so smart. She just took over. And Jess went along with everything she said. He had tried to make friends with them but it was a total waste of time. They treated him like he was some kind of moron.

"I'm going for a swim," he muttered. He stood up and immediately bumped his head on the rock roof of the cave. Bird laughed.

Pete ran out of the cave and plunged into the freezing green water of the lake. He swam around a corner of the rocks, pulled himself out of the water and sat on the warm granite. He pulled his knees tight to his chest. He heard claws scrabble on the rock above him and then Cousin jumped down on the rock next to him.

"Don't bug me, dog," he said. But Cousin put his paw on Pete's leg. Pete shoved it off. Cousin put it back. Pete shoved it off again.

"Jeez, dog, leave me alone."

But Cousin seemed to have his own ideas. He stared intently at Pete's face.

"I'm not a stupid cow. Quit trying to get me to go some-place."

Cousin didn't blink. He waited a few more minutes and when Pete didn't move, Cousin jumped back up the rock and trotted out of sight. Pete went on sitting. Maybe Bird and Jess would get tired of waiting for him and go home.

He sat there watching the water, the mountains and the long blue-green shadows on the mountains. A big purple grey and blue cloud was building up behind the mountain on the other side of the lake.

His grandmother had told him their names. "That's Castle Mountain," she said, "and that's Mt. McGregor. Nobody lives over on that side of the lake anymore, although they used to. Once there was a town over there. Now there's just a railway track that comes around the south end of the lake. See that hollow between the two mountains; just at the bottom is a long beach with fine white sand. It's at the mouth of a creek full of trout. Someday I'll take you there fishing. Oh it's so beautiful, Pete. Up above the beach, the creek has these big deep pools of green water with huge trout that have lived there forever. And down in that hollow between those two mountains is where the thunderstorms come."

A gust of wind hit his face and tugged at his hair. It felt good on his bare hot skin. The wind felt like fingers playing with his hair. The water in front of him began to crinkle up under the pressure from the wind. The lake was changing all over. It was like watching a play. He realized he could see the gusts of wind coming by the lines of colour they made on the lake. Where the wind hit, the water turned dark blue — he could hear the wind building strength, a distant roar like a waterfall. When he looked to the north, he saw that the lake water was a solid blue-black, topped by white tips. The waves were now beating on the rocks and nipping at his toes. A flash of lightning lit the purple-black cloud that was halfway across the sky. He wondered where Bird and Jess had gone. He should go find them but he was still too mad at them and too fascinated by this spectacle in front of him to leave.

The black line of waves and the roaring wind were coming closer and closer. It was like standing beside the tracks, waiting for a freight train. Then the wind hit him, cold, hard, whipping around his face and body; the waves in front of him were now crashing and banging against the rocks. The freezing spray splashed his bare legs. Thunder cracked and rolled across the valley. The lake had gone from flat calm to huge tossing waves in only a few minutes. Maybe this is what had happened to Pierre. If someone in a small boat got caught in the middle of the lake in such a storm, they wouldn't have a chance.

Lightning crackled again and Pete stood up. This was too much. Lightning was scary. It was time to head for home, the house, his grandma and some dinner. Rain slashed his shoulders as he stood up to leave. He scrambled over the rocks, checked in the cave for Bird and Jess but they had gone. At least his shirt and shoes were still there. He was shivering as he slipped them on.

"Nice, guys," he said out loud. "Run off without a word.

Some friends you are." He was seriously going to ignore them next time they came around, if they ever did.

He headed towards the beach but the rain was so hard now, he thought there might be some shelter under the trees. He climbed up into the forest away from the rocks and the storm. Although there was no real trail here, he was pretty sure he knew where he was going. He wanted to get away from the lightning. It would be safer under the trees. But once inside the line of trees, he realized how dark it had become.

It was getting pretty late, and the storm had eaten the last bit of light out of the sky. Shadows lurked under every rock or tree. It was quiet under the trees but far above, the wind roared and snarled in the treetops, which were bending and creaking. A branch crashed down somewhere near him. Oh, no, he thought, what if a tree came down on his head? He tried to go as fast as he could but without a path, he had to claw through bushes, scramble over downed logs, navigate up and down shelves of rock. He started worrying about bears again. He had asked his grandma about bears.

"Aren't they dangerous?" he had asked.

She laughed. "No, usually they are afraid of you; they can hear you coming and they get out of your way. Besides, Cousin will always let you know if there is a bear around."

So where the heck was Cousin when Pete needed him? Gone off with those traitors, Bird and Jess, probably.

He realized now he must have gone the wrong way,

gotten turned around somehow in the gloom. His grandma had said this area wasn't part of the farm. It was all trees. No one lived on this land although some rich guy from Calgary owned it. His stomach lurched. He turned around, headed back the way he thought he had come, but nothing looked familiar.

He stopped again, trying to think. He couldn't get too lost; he was somewhere between the lake and the highway. But it was very hard to tell where anything was in all this windy darkness. He began to hurry down a rocky slope, then his foot slipped on a boulder and suddenly he was tumbling over and over. He came to rest at the bottom of the slope, beside a huge rock. He lay there, trying to breathe, trying to tell if everything in his body still worked. Cautiously and painfully, he got to his feet. He seemed to be in a deep gully, surrounded by huge boulders and fallen trees. Feeling desperate, he began to follow the gully where it sloped down the hill. Surely it would lead back to the lake. He had to clamber over ancient fallen trees, where deadly spikes of broken branches stuck into the air, and then scramble over mossy giant rocks that seemed as if they were deliberately blocking his way.

Finally he crawled on his hands and knees onto a clear flat space. At the edge of this flat was a steep slope. If he was right about where he was going, the path to the farm should be at the bottom of this slope. Suddenly he stopped. His blood pounded in his ears. Something was moving through the trees. He strained his eyes. It was so hard to see. A crack of lightning lit up the forest. There was nothing there. He began to inch forward, trying to be quiet, trying to see whatever there was to see.

There it was again, a shape, a shadow. No, it looked like a man. He stood still, not even daring to breathe. Another lightning bolt. They were getting closer together. This time the thunder was almost deafening — there, a shadow of a man, moving away from him, going through the trees. Pete kept putting one foot in front of the other although he didn't want to; he wanted to find a place to hide, but he also wanted to get home to the safety of his grandma and the warm farmhouse.

He came out at the back of the old orchard with its ancient dying trees, covered in moss and tall grass and thistles reaching up to catch the branches in their thorny grasp. He had to wade through this sea of grass, some of which was taller than his head. But now, finally, he was on the path; now he could run as fast as he could to the farm — yet something, a noise, a crack of a branch made him turn around. There it was again, that shape. Was it a man or was it a shadow? And why did it look as if it were waving at him? Why was it so misty, wavy?

Pete backed away, felt the gravel and sand of the road under his feet, turned around, began to run, kept running as fast as he could, pounding his feet down hard, hard on the ground, even when his breath began to catch in his throat and his lungs felt like they were on fire, his ribs burning where he had smashed them on a rock — all the way to the warm lighted windows of the farmhouse. He slammed open the back door and almost fell inside,

And there was his grandma, having tea with Jess and Bird. Bird looked him up and down, took in his drenched clothes and wet hair and said calmly, "Hey, we were just getting worried. What happened to you? You look so scared. Did you see a ghost?"

Chapter Six

—

The next morning, after Pete had sat down for breakfast, his grandma turned to him. "Bird seems to have a lot of ideas about this gold-finding project. Listening to her makes me feel tired. She is an energetic young woman. Pretty, too. It's great you have her and Jess for friends."

Pete said nothing. Breakfast at his grandma's wasn't so strange anymore — he had told her he liked cornflakes for breakfast. There was usually some raspberries or strawberries or something to go with them. He concentrated on shovelling cornflakes into his mouth.

"You going over there today?"

"No," Pete said. He didn't look up.

"Oh."

The silence stretched on. Pete could hear a radio playing somewhere in the house, maybe upstairs in his grandma's room.

"You got anything else you want to do?" his grandma asked.

"Nope."

"Want to help me for a day?"

"Sure," he said. He wondered what she meant.

"There's always lots to do on a farm," she said cheerfully. "Garden needs weeding, raspberries need picking, sprinklers need moving, lawn needs mowing. Oh, right, and there's a hen with a new batch of chicks hatched out in the loft of the barn. We'll have to catch her and move her down into the chicken house. Well, let's get moving, off like a dirty shirt, as my dad, your great-grandpa, used to say."

Pete followed her outside. He spent the rest of the morning doing whatever she directed. He was curious about farming; he didn't know anything about it. In fact, he didn't know anyone else, besides his grandmother, who lived on a farm.

They came in at noon and his grandmother heated up some soup and set out some crackers and cheese. Pete slumped into a chair. His hair was covered in hay and dust; his hands felt like grubby lumps covered with dirt, his shiny new clothes were smeared with mud. They had chased the chicken around the loft of the barn; it screeched and fought while they tried to herd the tiny balls of fluff that were the new baby chicks into a box.

After that was accomplished, they moved several sprinklers around under the apple trees. This involved walking through the spray, grabbing the sprinkler, moving it as fast as you could, and then running away before you got drenched. In the process, Pete discovered, you got drenched.

Then they weeded the garden, picked some raspberries and soon it was time for lunch. Pete gobbled down his soup, wondering what torture his grandmother had planned for the afternoon.

"Okay," she said, "now I'm going to have a nap and then I have a letter I need to write. You're on your own for the afternoon."

"Grandma," Pete said.

"Yes, dear heart?"

"Do you still write books and stuff?"

She went very still. Then she sighed. "No," she said, "I haven't written anything new for a long time."

"Are you famous?"

"I was a little bit famous, once, for a little while. It was fun. But it didn't last."

"Bird thinks you're a great poet. She says her dad says you are brilliant."

"That is very kind of her."

"So why don't you write a new book?"

"Because for a new book, I need new ideas. And I don't have any." Her face twisted. She looked like she might cry again.

"I'm sorry, Grandma," Pete said in alarm. It scared him when she cried.

"Honey, it's not your fault. You are the most wonderful gift to me, and your visit here this summer has made me feel better than anything else has for a long, long time. By the way, there's some ice cream in the fridge."

He heard her determined step on the stairs and then the bed creaked as she lay down.

He filled a bowl with ice cream and went outside to sit on the steps. Cousin sat in front of him and pleaded with his eyes, so when Pete was only half-done, he put the bowl down and let Cousin lick it clean.

He sat with his head in his hands, thinking about the previous evening. What had he seen in the woods? He had been so scared that he couldn't even remember it properly. All he remembered was a misty shape that looked like it was waving at him.

When Bird had made her crack about seeing a ghost, he had walked right past her and into his room and slammed the door. He didn't come out until he heard Bird and Jess leaving. His grandmother hadn't said anything about him being rude, just dished him up some food and talked a bit about the storm. She said they got a lot of storms like this in the summer. "If you're out in a boat and you see that black line coming, head for shore," she warned.

He realized now he was going to have to go back there and look. In the daylight, with the sun shining, the idea didn't seem so scary.

"C'mon, Cousin," he said. "Stick with me. Where were you yesterday when I needed you?"

Together they loped down the road towards the lake. When they got to the place where the path wound down through the dark trees to the beach, Pete turned and started through the orchard into the thick, dark woods. As they entered the darkness under the trees, Pete's feet slowed and stopped all by themselves. But Cousin ran on ahead and disappeared. Pete started his feet moving again, although it was hard and they seemed to be going very slowly.

When he came to an enormous rock covered with green and grey mounds of moss, he stopped again, peering into the gloom. It was so silent under the trees. It was hard to move and break the silence. Long thin pencils of sunlight slanted down and dappled the grey trunks of the firs. Cousin came back, snuffling along the ground. When he saw Pete, he waved his tail in acknowledgement but went on checking out the smells of the forest. Pete got himself going again. He went slowly towards the place where he thought he had seen the figure but there was no sign of anything strange. He kept going through the trees, towards the place he thought he had been the previous evening. He stopped and listened intently. He heard squirrels chattering away, one after another, from tree to tree, like some kind of crazy alarm system. Maybe that's what it was. Maybe they were announcing him. A raven flew silently into a tree ahead of him and then slid out again without making a sound.

I've never been in the woods alone before, Pete thought to himself. He had gone on hikes with his parents or with a school group, gone camping, gone to parks, but he was always protected inside a noisy group. Stepping into these woods was like stepping into a big green silent castle, or what he had always imagined a castle would be like.

But he couldn't seem to find the strange gully he knew he had been in. He found the flat place he remembered after scrambling up a cliff where he had to hold on to roots and rocks and dig his feet into the sandy crumbling soil. But every time he tried to leave it, he either ran into a tangle of brush or a steep unclimbable cliff.

He stood still, staring all around him, listening to the silence. Then Cousin came crawling out from what had looked like an impenetrable tangle of trees. When Pete went to look, he realized that a whole lot of trees were tangled together in some odd way but there seemed to be a space if he could just crawl through underneath them. He made it, and there were the huge boulders he remembered piled in a steep gully. He followed the gully downwards and then suddenly stopped.

A pine tree had crashed down onto the bank; its tangle of roots was sticking up in the air, while the branches had splintered and broken on impact. Pete clambered over the trunk then stopped suddenly and stared. Where the roots had torn free of the ground was a small black space, a hole of some kind only about a foot high. Pete inched closer.

It was like a cave, only there were logs holding up the entrance. They looked really old. One had buckled in half, but was still hanging there with the ends stuck in the dirt. He peered into the black mouth of the cave, his heart pounding. He had to get on his hands and knees to squeeze inside, but once inside he could stand up. He took one step into the darkness, then another and another.

When he had taken about ten steps into the cave, it was already too dark to see. It smelled damp and mouldy. It probably wasn't safe. What if it collapsed on him? Suddenly the tunnel seemed very narrow. He began panting, sucking in air. He turned and ran for the light and crawled back out the hole. Cousin was waiting outside for him and gave him a disapproving look.

Pete sat down on a rock, thinking hard. This tunnel might be something Pierre had made. Maybe it was where he had hidden his gold. It was hard to breathe for the excitement. He needed to look inside but it was too dark.

He looked at the pine tree. How long did it take pine trees to grow? Maybe this tree hadn't even been here when Pierre was here. He peered inside again. He needed to come back with a good flashlight. Maybe he should talk to Bird and Jess and tell them what he had found. Then he thought about how bossy Bird was and how Jess followed her around like a dopey puppy. Forget it, he told himself. This was his secret for now. When he found the lost gold, then he could swagger in, announce his find in triumph. That would shut Bird and Jess up for good.

It was still early afternoon. Maybe he could go ask his grandma for a flashlight, make some excuse that he needed it for the other cave at the beach.

It took him a long time, even though he trotted all the way back to the house, puffing and panting in the heat while Cousin loped at his heels. When he got back to the house, it was quiet. His grandma must still be sleeping. He tiptoed upstairs and stopped in her doorway. She was curled up on the bed, sound asleep. She looked sad, sleeping like that. It made him feel strange. She had been so nice to him. In the last couple of days, his feelings about being at the farm had changed. He especially liked listening to his grandma tell stories about the old days. It made him feel funny inside, both sad and excited at the same time.

And no matter what he did, she seemed to think it was interesting. He had even talked to her a little bit about school, and his friends, and how it made him crazy when his mom fussed at him all the time. She just listened and nodded like it all made perfect sense.

He turned and tiptoed back down the stairs. Then he remembered — there was a flashlight in the barn. He had noticed it the day she showed him the two brown and white cows with their baby calves. The cows weren't very friendly, and his grandma said they only came in the barn at night to get some hay. But the calves were cute. They had licked his hands and sniffed at his shoes.

He headed for the barn with Cousin at his heels. But when he got there, the flashlight was gone. He sighed in impatience. He'd just have to wait until his grandma woke up. He turned and scrambled up the ladder into the hayloft. Squatting on his heels, he could see out over the pasture, where the cows were grazing beside the cedar pole fence that his grandma said had been built by Pierre.

What had that been like, he wondered, to come here when there was nothing but trees and then, somehow, to make a farm and a house? Pierre had been eighteen, only six years older than he was. He tried to imagine the pasture covered with trees. How had Pierre managed to cut them all down and build a house and a barn and everything else? How did you even start building a house? Pete had no idea. He wondered if Pierre had been lonely. He had left all of his family behind in France.

And then Pete's great-great-grandfather had lived here, and his great-grandfather and then his grandfather and his father. He had never really thought about that before. They had probably squatted right here, as he was doing, and looked out at the farm. That was an amazing thought. Why hadn't his dad told him about the story of the farm? Everyone in Victoria that Pete knew was from somewhere else. His best friend Niko had moved to Victoria from Romania. His other friend, Justin, was from Africa.

Maybe Bird was right. Maybe the farm shouldn't be sold. If other people built houses here, they wouldn't know anything about Pierre or his grandfather or his great-grandfather. They wouldn't care. But did that really matter? His grandma and Bird seemed to think it did; his mom and dad obviously thought it didn't. So how did he feel about it? He stopped. He thought about the farm disappearing under condos and a hotel and, to his amazement, he felt a rush of fury. "What about me?" he said out loud. He realized he liked feeling a part of something. He was starting to get a sense of what his grandmother felt.

It was so quiet. He could hear distant things in the quietness, things he had never noticed before, like the sound of a distant raven. A little breeze came and lifted his hair and shivered the limbs of the huge cedar tree beside the barn. He noticed the sound it made, like a soft sigh, then the sudden smell of hot cedar and dust and cow manure from the barn. For a moment, he felt strange, as if he were someone else, someone a lot older.

Suddenly, he saw Cousin trotting towards the house and he heard the sound of a door slamming. His grandma must be awake. He slid down the ladder and headed towards the house.

"Peter," she called. She was standing by the picnic table. "Popcorn and root beer. C'mon, picnic time."

He laughed to himself. His crazy grandma. She loved junk food. She just said, "I'm too old to worry about what

I eat. Food is for fun, Pete, not for worrying about." But he figured it was probably okay since she also made sure they ate lots of fresh fruit and vegetables from her garden. Vegetables tasted different when they were fresh. One day he had helped his grandma pick a whole bowl of peas, and then they ate them raw for supper. That was fun.

He plunked himself down at the picnic table and dug in. He wanted to ask his grandma a question but he had to assemble all the words in his head first. He knew now that she would wait patiently for him to get it all sorted out.

"Grandma?" he said, but he didn't have it quite organized yet. It was a big thought. She waited.

"So, all that stuff about Pierre and my great-great-grandpa and this farm. That's like real history, right?"

She nodded.

"So how come it's so interesting and all that history stuff we get in school is boring?"

She thought for a moment. "It depends on how you look at things, Pete. If you think of history as real stories that happened to real people, and you talk about it or read about it that way, then it's almost as if it happened to you. You can relate to it."

He thought about that for a while. It made sense.

"Did Pierre have a mine of his own?" he asked.

"He probably did. It was mostly miners who were the first white people to come into this country. For a while, people were digging holes all over these mountains. Some found gold and silver, but many of them didn't find anything. A few of them made fortunes, but mostly, they went broke."

"Do you think Pierre found some gold?"

"No, I don't think so. When you have a mine, you have to register it with the government. It's called a mining claim and as far as I know, he never did that. I think he mostly won his gold playing poker."

"Grandma," he said again. "Can I borrow a flashlight?"

"Sure," she said. "There's one in the cupboard in the kitchen. I keep it there for emergencies. Just put it back when you're done with it."

She didn't ask him why he wanted it. He thought of telling her about the mysterious tunnel he had found. But it was so great to have a secret; he wanted to keep it to himself for just a little while longer. It was too late to go exploring today. He'd go tomorrow and take Cousin.

That night after supper, they lit a fire in the fireplace, even though it wasn't cold.

"Fires are for stories," his grandmother said.

"Tell me another story about Pierre," Pete asked.

"Well," said his grandmother, "actually there are lots of stories about him. He was pretty crazy. You see, in those days, there was no road to this farm. There was a kind of wagon trail, called the tote road, but all the buildings were on the other side of the lake because that's where the railroad was and because there were a whole bunch of mines over there. Some man who was lost actually stumbled over a boulder full of silver, and once he announced his discovery, the rush was on. The miners who came found silver and lead and copper but only a little gold. Across the lake, there used to be a whole town called Silver City. It had hotels and bars, an opera house, a church and a school and all kinds of things. Pierre used to row across the lake to play poker and drink and visit the ladies."

"How far is it?"

"About three miles. It's amazing that he never drowned, rowing back at night, drunk, in the dark. But he was tough. He used to get into fights too, apparently."

"So what happened to the city?"

"There was a fire and most of it burned down. Several people died in the fire. And eventually, when the mines ran out of ore, the city was abandoned. They were mining a kind of silver ore called galena. The biggest mine was following a vein of ore that ran down under the lake. One day they blasted through the wall between the mine and the lake and the whole thing flooded. Several miners drowned. So gradually the mines shut down, and the city, what was left of it, disappeared, covered over with trees and brush. It's absolutely amazing how fast nature eats up the evidence of civilization. You can still find old bottles and bits and pieces of iron and machines hiding under the trees. It's a ghost city now. But if you look, you can find evidence of the mines all over the hills on both sides of the lake. There's lots of old diggings and mine shafts. But they're dangerous, Pete; they can collapse. If you find one, don't go inside it."

"Where did the miners come from?"

"Oh, from all over. Most of them were young men, but women came too. A lot of the miners came from the United States, some from England, or Europe. That's why they mostly used gold coins for money. In fact, some people in Silver City made their own gold coins. A lot of the miners got killed in accidents or they got lost in the mountains. They mostly travelled here on the rivers and lakes.

"You see, Pete, in those days, there weren't any roads, so the railways built lines into the mountains to ship out the ore, and they also built big boats called sternwheelers that went up and down the lake. If you put out a flag or a sign, they would stop. We used to have a flag here to stop the boat. It's still up in the attic if you want to see it. My granddad used to ship boxes of apples to market on the sternwheeler. They would stop at any beach where there was a house or a sign. Sternwheelers were very flat on the bottom so the captain would just run the front of the boat up on the beach and then back off again. The sternwheelers even used to have races. I've got a book of pictures upstairs, if you're interested."

"Cool," said Pete.

"I didn't know you liked all this history stuff," she said, smiling at him.

"Well, it's different the way you tell it."

"Well, I've got lots more stories, but right now it's my bedtime. You can stay up if you want. Or I'll fetch that book of pictures and you can take it to bed with you."

Chapter Seven

—

The next morning at breakfast his grandma said, "Bird phoned. She wants you to come over."

Pete shifted uncomfortably in his chair. He didn't want to talk to Bird, but his grandma seemed to think Bird was so great. Beside, he had to go explore the tunnel.

"She's bossy," he muttered.

"She's a girl," his grandma said. "All girls are bossy. Plus she's really smart, just like you. She and Jess were worried that you'd think they were just stupid country kids. They thought you'd be a big snob who would make fun of them."

He stared at her. Him the big snob? They were the snobby ones.

"Anyway, she says she has something important to talk to you about. It's up to you, though."

Pete shrugged. His heart sank. "Okay," he sighed. His mom always told him to not be rude, to be nice to people. Plus he didn't want his grandma to think he was a jerk.

He went to his room and changed into his coolest black t-shirt and jeans. Then he combed his hair with gel so it would stick up properly. When he came out of the bathroom his grandma said, "Wow, you look great! What a handsome grandson I have," and even though he knew it was silly, he kind of liked hearing it.

He decided to stop at Jess's house before he went to Bird's, and see if Jess would come with him. No way he wanted to go to Bird's house and be there with her all by himself. He set off on his bike but he had only made it to the top of the first hill when a big black SUV whooshed by him. He stopped his bike and stared behind him. It looked like the car belonging to that real estate guy but he couldn't be sure. Should he go back?

Finally, he began pedalling again. When he reached the bottom of Jess's driveway, he had to stop and push his bike up the long steep hill. Mosquitoes flew around his head and whined near his nose and ears but he couldn't stop long enough to fight them off. When he got to the top of the hill, no one was home. He banged on the door, looked in the windows, sat down on the doorstep, trying to decide what to do next. Bird's house was another long mile in the summer heat. The mosquitoes wouldn't leave him alone. He couldn't keep sitting here. He'd be eaten alive.

Feeling discouraged, he climbed on his bike and roared down the hill, almost becoming airborne over the bumps and holes in the driveway. At the bottom, by the highway, he hesitated again. He could go back to his grandma's, and pretend he had never made the trip at all. He could make some excuse to his grandma but what would he say? If he said Bird wasn't home, she'd soon find out that wasn't true.

He pedalled slowly along the road towards Bird's house. At last he reached her driveway, got off his bike and pushed his way up another long hill. Why did everyone who lived here have a long steep driveway? In the pasture, the horses trotted up to the white rail fence, snorting and then running away, tossing their dark beautiful heads.

There was a car in the driveway and the sound of music coming from the house. Pete sighed with relief. At least one of her parents was home. They could sit around and be polite and then he could leave. Perhaps he could talk Bird's mother or father into giving him a ride back to the farm. He banged on the door and waited. A tall man came to the door and looked out. Pete gulped.

"Is Bird, umm, I mean, Robin home?" His voice came out squeaky and high. He had dust in his throat; he coughed and then couldn't stop coughing.

"You'd better come in and have a drink of water," said the man, looking concerned. "Bird isn't here. She went to town with her mom but she should be back any moment. Is it important?"

"No," Pete gasped. He took the glass of water and gulped it down. That made him choke, so then he was coughing and choking while the man pounded him on his back.

"You'd better sit down," the man said. "Did you ride all this way in the heat? You might have heat stroke. You're Avery's grandson, aren't you? I've seen your picture in her house. I'm Robin's dad. My name is Robert. Call me Rob." Pete sank into a chair, feeling like an idiot. He remembered that Bird's dad was a doctor.

"Maybe I should take your temperature," Rob said. "Maybe you should lie down. Do you want me to call your grandmother?"

"No, it's okay," Pete muttered. The cough was going away now and he was getting his voice back.

He and Bird's father sat together in silence.

"I kind of needed to talk to Bird," he said.

"Well, you're welcome to wait."

"What time is it?"

"A little after ten."

Pete hesitated. "I'd better go," he said. "Tell Bird I'll call her later."

"I'll give you a ride," Rob said. "I've been wanting a chance to say hello to your grandmother. She's one of my favourite patients."

"Thanks," Pete said. He was too tired and fed up to argue. It was just like Bird to phone him and tell him to come over and then not even wait around to see if he would show up.

Outside, they loaded Pete's bike into the back of Rob's

brand new Jeep Cherokee. Pete thought about how his mother always said people with big sport utility vehicles were destroying the planet but didn't say anything. He was just glad for the ride.

"So are you having a good summer?" Rob asked.

"It's okay."

"Your grandma is a wonderful woman. I've known her since I moved to the valley. I used to read her poetry when I first went to university. Have you read any of it?"

"Nope." He hated it when grown-ups asked questions. But nothing seemed to discourage this guy. No wonder Bird talked all the time.

"Well, it's sure great that you and Robin and Jess are friends. Jess is a great kid. Robin tells me you guys all went swimming together the other day. She said you had a great picnic down at the beach."

"Kind of." Would the guy never shut up?

"I remember when I went to the beach as a kid. We got up to all kinds of stuff. We used to build forts out of driftwood, and smoke cigarettes we stole from our parents. I bet you guys have tried that too."

Now Pete was shocked.

"I don't smoke," he said.

"Well, that's a good thing," Rob said. "I told Robin if she ever wanted to smoke, I'd buy her some cigarettes and she'd have to try it first in front of me and then I'd tell her just how bad they are for you. She never took me up on the offer. Well, here we are. I'm going to come in and say hello to Avery. I haven't seen her for a while."

They unloaded Pete's bike and Pete wheeled it into the shed. Rob went on ahead into the house.

Pete followed. But once inside, there was no sign of his grandmother.

"Grandma," he called. There was no answer. "Maybe she's in the garden," he said to Rob.

But Rob wasn't listening to Pete; instead he was listening to some other noise, a kind of soft moan. Then he was bounding up the stairs.

Pete ran after him.

"Avery," Rob called. "Avery? Oh, my goodness."

Pete's grandmother was on the floor and Rob was kneeling beside her, his hand on her wrist, taking her pulse. Then he had his cellphone out, speaking urgently. "This is Dr. Dillon. I need an ambulance. Yes, Highway 31, the fire number is 9941. Yes, an elderly female, pulse 160, I don't have a BP. I'll be right here, hurry."

Pete stood in the doorway feeling helpless. His hands dangled at his sides. His throat swelled closed. It ached with the yell building inside him.

"Grandma," he wanted to yell. "Grandma," but he didn't say a word.

"Pete, get a blanket and a pillow," snapped Rob. "She needs to be kept warm and comfortable. See if you can get her to talk. If you can, keep her talking, keep her awake. I'm going out to the car — I've got my bag with a blood pressure cuff in the back."

Pete stumbled towards the bed, his feet feeling two sizes too big. He grabbed a quilt and a pillow, knelt beside his grandma to slip the pillow under her head.

"Pete," she said softly, without opening her eyes.

"Grandma?"

"Oh, my dearest little Petey," she sighed. She opened her eyes and stared at him and then her eyes closed again.

Petey was what she had always called him when he was little. "Grandma," he said. "Grandma, you're supposed to stay awake. Please wake up, please, Grandma."

"You talk to me," she said drowsily. Her words slurred a little. "Tell me stories, tell me dreams. There's a black place . . ." her voice trailed off.

"What black place? Grandma, what happened? Did you fall?"

"That man," she said. Her voice was thin and whispery. "He called me an old fool. Well, so I am but I don't need him reminding me. I came upstairs to phone Fern, and then I stumbled, hit my head. Oh, my side hurts."

She fumbled with her hand towards her side and Pete took her hand in his. It felt fragile, thin and cold.

She was silent again. Pete went on holding her hand, trying to think of what to say. He was supposed to keep talking. He felt so useless. What could he say? "Grandma, you're going to be okay," he said. "They're sending an ambulance.

Rob is going to take your blood pressure and when the ambulance guys get here, everything will be fine. I'll take care of the chickens and the cats and Cousin. Don't worry about anything. And don't worry about the farm. If that guy shows up, Cousin and I will take care of him."

"Pete, you are the best kid in the world," she whispered. Her voice sounded a bit stronger.

"Okay," said Rob, coming back into the room. "Good job. She's looking better already. When someone has an accident, it's important to keep the patient warm; it keeps them from going into shock."

"She says her side hurts," Pete said.

"Right, maybe a cracked rib. Okay, Avery, let's have a look." Rob took a blood pressure reading then checked Pete's grandma for injuries.

"Nothing too serious," he concluded cheerfully. "But we'll need an x-ray to know for sure. A cracked rib or two, a bump on the head, maybe a bit of concussion. Looks like a hospital stay for you, Avery."

"I hate that place," Grandma said. She was waking up. Her eyes had begun to look normal but her voice still sounded shaky. "I'll go have the x-ray but then I'm coming home."

"I'm glad to hear your fighting spirit, Avery. I'd be really worried if you were happy about going to the hospital. But I think you might have to stay overnight. Pete can stay with us until you come home."

Pete looked at his grandma and she looked back at him.

"Rob, I can't leave the animals alone. Pete knows all the chores. Can't he stay here during the day? He is a very capable, mature boy."

"By himself? I don't think that's a good idea."

"I'll be okay," Pete said.

"He'll be fine," his grandma said, her voice growing a bit stronger. "If you and Fern can arrange to feed him, maybe bring a few pizzas and some pepperoni over, he'll survive. Oh, and ice cream. He's a growing boy, he's got to have a supply of ice cream."

Rob shook his head but he didn't argue anymore.

When the ambulance arrived, they let Pete ride in the back with his grandmother. The ambulance driver turned on the siren and they raced down the highway towards the hospital. The ride scared Pete even more than the sight of his grandmother lying so still. He held on as they swayed around corners and swerved around cars. He could hear the two guys up front talking and laughing, and he guessed no one was in any danger, but it sure felt dangerous. His grandma lay quietly with her eyes closed but a couple of times she reached out and patted his hand.

When they reached the hospital, the ambulance attendants wheeled her inside, and then nurses in white coats put his grandma on another stretcher and took her away. No one paid any attention to him. Pete was left standing in an ugly, cramped, yellow room with a few chairs and a table with a bunch of old magazines, mostly about cooking. He sat down, leafed disinterestedly through an ancient edition of *People* magazine. He stood up, stared out the window, sat back down again. His stomach growled and he realized with a shock that he was hungry. It felt wrong to be hungry while his grandma was lying in the hospital.

Then suddenly Fern came hurrying in the door with Jess and Bird right behind her. He was so glad to see them he forgot about being mad at them.

Bird threw her arms around him and hugged him. It was embarrassing but it felt good as well.

"Hey man," said Jess, patting him awkwardly on the shoulder. "Your grandma, man, that's tough. What happened? Did she trip or something? Is she going to be okay?"

"She's got some cracked ribs or something. She fell. It was that guy, that real-estate guy, or whatever he is. She got so mad, she didn't look where she was going."

"Where were you?" Bird said.

"On my way to see you," Pete said. He stared at her.

"Oh, no," she said. "That's right. You must think I'm so rude. I'm sorry I wasn't home. My mom made me go with her and I forgot to phone. I was going to phone you as soon as I got back and tell you to come over later."

"Pete," said Fern. "I'll bet you haven't had any lunch. What say I swing by a restaurant, pick up some burgers and fries and come back here. We can eat outside on the lawn while we wait to hear about your grandma."

"Hey, thanks," Pete said. Fern took all their orders and left. Pete sat down and Bird and Jess sat on either side of him.

"I'm sorry, Pete," Bird said. "Is there anything we can do? Where are you going to stay?"

"At the farm," Pete said.

"By yourself? You can't."

"Yes, I can. It's sort of like my farm too. I have to look after everything. Grandma asked me to."

"We'll come and help," said Jess. "We can pick stuff or feed the chickens or whatever. Hey, how hard can that be?"

He looked at them. Maybe he'd been wrong about them. He kind of understood now that his grandma had explained it, that they would have been showing off for someone coming from the big city. Maybe they had thought that, because he was so quiet, he didn't like them.

He hesitated, planning his words. "I've got something to show you," he said at last. "I found a kind of tunnel place, maybe an old mine, where a tree fell down in that last storm. I looked in but I couldn't see anything. It was too dark."

The words came running and tumbling over themselves now. He tried to stop them or slow them down but he couldn't. "I think there might be something hidden there. It looks like someone made it a long time ago. I think it's Pierre's mine. Grandma said he had one. So that might be where the gold is hidden."

"Wow, we've got to go look, right away," Jess said.

"It might be dangerous," Bird said. "Maybe we should tell someone first."

"No, don't tell anyone," Pete said. "I want it to be a surprise for Grandma. We'll go tomorrow. We'll need ropes, a flashlight, shovels, maybe some other stuff."

"That is so great," Bird said. She was looking at him with admiration. Pete took a deep breath. He felt the heat in his face and he knew his cheeks and probably his ears were turning red but he didn't care.

"Oh, no," Bird said, "I just remembered, I can't go tomorrow, I have this piano recital. It's a big deal, I can't get out of it, I've been practising for weeks."

"Oh, right, and I've got a swimming competition," said Jess.

"That's okay," Pete said. "I've got stuff to take care of. You know — the farm, the animals, all that stuff."

"Are you really going to take care of everything all by yourself?" asked Bird. "That is so brave, Pete. Looking after your grandma's house and all those animals. We'll come as soon as we can, I promise. Don't do anything fun without us, okay?"

"Sure," said Pete, already thinking how great it would be to find the gold all by himself, to be the triumphant hero, the one who saved the day, saved the farm, saved his grandma, and got Jess and Bird's admiration into the bargain.

Fern arrived with the hamburgers and drinks, and Pete

realized he was starved. The food disappeared quickly. Just as they were finishing, Rob came out and said Pete could see his grandma. Afterwards, Rob would drive him home to the farm.

Pete tiptoed into the room, but his grandma was sitting up in bed. She looked pale and her hair was sticking up in odd little spikes.

"Hey, grandma, are you okay?"

"Of course. A few cracked ribs are nothing serious. They fix themselves. I'll be home tomorrow. Petey, my dearest boy, are you sure you will be okay on your own?"

"Yes, I'll be fine. It'll be cool. My mom would so totally not approve."

"Hmmm," she said and grinned all over her face. "So, will I get into big trouble?"

He grinned back. "Probably."

"Pete, can you do me a big favour?"

"Sure, of course."

"Go borrow a pen and some paper from the nurse. I need to write some stuff down. Lying here has got me thinking."

"Okay."

He went back out in the hall. It took a while until he found a passing nurse who would let him have a few sheets of paper and a pen. He took them back to his grandma, said goodbye to her, and then Rob drove him home to the silent empty farmhouse.

Chapter Eight

—

"I still don't think it's a good idea for you to be here by yourself," Rob said after he had parked the Jeep. "I'm sure your mother and father would never allow it. Why don't I drop you off at home for the rest of the afternoon, then we'll come up and do the chores after supper."

Pete looked at the floor. Where were the right words when he really needed them? He wanted to say that he'd be fine on his own. He wanted to stay here. His grandma had asked him to. He wanted to explore this new feeling of possession and connection he'd felt in the barn a few days earlier. Being alone made him feel, for the first time, as if he were really, finally growing up.

"My mom wouldn't mind," he said finally. Even to his own ears, it sounded lame. "Grandma wants me to."

Rob shook his head. "Well, we can argue about this later. I can see you're determined. You're a lot like your grandmother, young fella. But I've got to get going. I should have been at the clinic two hours ago. I'll be back later to pick you up."

After Rob left, Pete sat in the empty kitchen by himself for a long time. It was already late afternoon. The sun was slanting in long rays through the windows. The house made strange creaking noises as it settled around him. He could hear the swallows under the eaves as they flew in and out feeding their babies. He was suddenly exhausted. He went to his room and curled up on the bed. Cousin flopped onto the floor beside the bed. The grey cat sprawled beside him. He stared at a comic book for a while but the words didn't make any sense.

Finally, he got up and wandered out to the kitchen. He looked in the fridge for food, decided that a bowl of raspberries, cherries and a glass of chocolate milk sounded good, then went outside with Cousin bounding beside him. He fed the chickens, checked on the hen with the new baby chicks, emptied the compost bucket, and washed the dishes. As he finished the last of the dishes, the phone rang. It was Fern, checking up on him.

"Do you need me to come over?" she asked.

"No, Rob is coming later," he said. And yes, he added in response to her questions, the animals were fine and he was fine and the farm was fine and yes, he had lots to eat.

As he hung up the phone it rang again; this time it was Rob.

"I'm tied up at the hospital for now," he said. "There's been a car accident. I'll have to come out later to get you. I might be pretty late. Do you have something for supper?" Rob sounded as though he was in a big hurry.

"It's okay, I'm fine. Fern said she would come over later."

"Oh, Fern is coming? Okay, I won't worry about you. Okay, I'll be right there," he yelled to someone else. The phone clicked in Pete's ear.

As he hung up the phone it rang a third time.

"Hello," he said this time with irritation.

"Hey son, what's going on?"

"Dad!"

"How's your grandma? What is going on there? Some doctor called me, said your grandma was in the hospital. Who is there looking after everything?"

"Grandma's fine," Pete said. "She fell down. She's in the hospital overnight. I'm taking care of things."

There was a brief silence. "You?" said his father "You're taking care of things? By yourself?"

"Yeah," said Pete.

"Speak up, Pete, I can hardly hear you. Do you need me to come out there? I can try and get there as fast as I can but it's difficult. I'm in Moscow. I probably couldn't get a flight until tomorrow or the next day. I'd have to rearrange my whole schedule. Are you sure you're going to be okay? I just talked to your mom and she is going to fly out as soon as she can but it might be hard to get a flight right away. It's Africa, after all."

"I'm fine, Dad, really," Pete said. But his father didn't hear him. He was still talking.

"Just hang on, son. I'll call the hospital later, and if I really need to, somehow, I'll get there. Remember, I love you. Bye now."

Pete hung up the phone very carefully.

"I'm fine," he said loudly to the now silent phone. "I'm fine, I'm fine, I'm fine, okay? I can truly, actually, really take care of myself."

He went back and lay down on the bed. After a while, he got up, brushed his teeth, climbed into his pajamas and got into bed. Cousin curled up on the rug beside him and both cats jumped on the bed and lay on top of him, purring. The house was full of strange noises he had never noticed before, but soon, his eyes drooped and he fell asleep.

He woke up just as the light was turning grey and the birds were starting to chirp from the trees, and then he fell asleep again. Just as he was coming awake, caught somewhere between dreaming and waking, he felt the bed bounce underneath him. Maybe Cousin had jumped on the bed, he thought drowsily.

"Cousin, get off," he muttered. "Go lie down."

But the bed bounced again, even more violently — he opened his eyes and sat up. Suddenly Pete caught his breath and his heart pounded in his chest. There was a face in the window, the face of a man with black hair and dark eyes. His mouth was open; he seemed to be saying something.

Pete rubbed his eyes, and then opened them again. The face was gone. He looked around. Neither Cousin nor the cats were on the bed. Pete fell back on the pillows and closed his eyes. He lay there thinking about all the events of the past week, about his grandma, about Bird and Jess and about how he was going to find the rest of the gold.

He thought again about the face he had seen in the window. He wanted to tell someone about it. He wished he could tell his grandmother about it. She might say it was all just a dream but at least she would take it seriously.

He stood up, pulled on the same clothes he had worn yesterday, stumbled out to the kitchen and poured some cornflakes and milk in a bowl. After he had eaten, he fed the cats and Cousin. He went outside and searched through the garage for a shovel and a rope. He found a shovel in the garden shed and went to look in the barn for a rope. Then he came back in the house and got the flashlight and a canvas bag to put everything in. At the last moment, he added some matches and a package of pepperoni. After that, he had a bowl of ice cream and raspberries before leaving.

As he was opening the back door, the phone rang again. Reluctantly, Pete dropped the bag of tools and ran to grab the phone.

"Darling, oh my poor sweetie, are you okay?"

Pete sighed. "Yes, Mom, I'm fine." His heart sank. His mother had gotten too used to running everything as if it were her classes, her university department. Sometimes he wondered if she forgot that he wasn't just another wayward student.

"Speak up, sweetheart, I can hardly hear you. How is your grandma?"

"She's okay," he said. "The doctor says she'll be fine."

"And so who is looking after you? Who is at the house with you?"

"Well, no one right now."

"What? What do you mean, no one? You mean you are there all by yourself?"

"Well, just for now."

"What do you mean, just for now?"

"Well, someone is coming by pretty soon."

"Who, Petey, who is coming and when are they coming?"

"Rob and Fern. They're grandma's neighbours." He crossed his fingers. He wasn't really lying to his mother. They would both be over later, sometime, especially when they figured out he had lied to both of them.

"Dad phoned," he said, to distract her.

"Oh, your father," she answered. "Yes, he called to tell me about your grandma. He thinks he should leave the tour and go take care of both of you. But he wouldn't be able to get there for a week. I'm sorry, Peter. It was obviously a mistake to send you there. It was too much of a burden for your grandmother."

"No, Mom, it's okay. We're getting along great. Grandma just has some cracked ribs. She'll be home soon."

"And then who is going to look after both of you? No Peter, you will have to come back to Victoria as soon as I can arrange something. I'll have to hire someone, I guess. Or maybe there's a summer camp you could go to."

Pete took a deep breath. "No," he said, "I'm fine. I'm staying here with Grandma. She needs me."

There was a long silence on the other end of the line. He waited. Then she said, "Peter, what has gotten into you?"

"I like it here," he said.

"I'm sure your grandmother has filled your head with a lot of romantic nonsense about that old farm. But she is going to need some proper care, more than you can provide. Maybe your father and I can arrange to hire a nurse."

Peter felt his heart sink. His mother might as well be on a different planet. What had happened to her? She used to be so great. When he was little, they used to have such a good time together. Now she was this bossy stranger.

"I can help her," he mumbled.

"You, the boy who can't make his bed or wash a dish by himself? I'd like to see that."

"Mom, just wait, okay, please." His voice cracked.

Another silence. This time her voice had softened. "Okay, Peter, I'll talk to your father and your grandmother about it all. By the way, are you wearing your hat and sunscreen and taking your vitamins? I suppose your grandmother has been spoiling you rotten and you've forgotten entirely how to behave."

"Mom, I have to go, I think I hear a car. Someone is coming."

"All right. But I'll call again later. Bye, my darling. Peter, please remember I love you and I only want the best for you. I need to know that you're safe."

"Bye Mom." Pete slammed the phone into the receiver. He was sorry about lying to his mother but talking to her made him crazy. It was time to get out of the house before anyone else called or arrived or figured out some other way to distract him.

He set out for the tunnel at a trot with Cousin at his heels. The shovel banged awkwardly at his side. The morning sun was lighting everything. Tiny drops of dew sparkled on the grass. It was so beautiful that Pete stopped to look around. The sun was just hitting the tops of the mountains across the lake. The little bit of snow that was left on their tops glowed bright pink. On the mountain behind him, the trees were outlined in light, as if they were lit from inside. Amazing, he thought.

But when he finally reached the dark opening of the tunnel, he hesitated. He could just imagine what his mother would say about this. She'd have a fit. He crouched on his hands and knees and shone the flashlight inside the tunnel mouth, but the darkness seemed to devour the tiny beam of light. After a long moment, he sighed, got down on his hands and knees and crawled inside, dragging the shovel behind him. Once inside, he turned on the flashlight again, and stood up, flashing the light over the walls, the dirt above his head, the rocky walls. All he could see was dirt and rocks. The rocks were a funny kind of white and grey colour. They shone in the light from his flashlight but there was nothing that looked like gold.

The muddy cave floor slanted steeply upwards as he walked farther. He stopped and looked back. The mouth of the cave seemed far away, a round flat plate of light and sun. He stepped carefully over piles of rocks on the floor of the tunnel until even the last vestige of light disappeared. He turned off the flashlight for a second. It was amazing. It was truly pitch black. He couldn't see a thing. He turned the light back on and took a few more steps. The tunnel ended abruptly at what looked like a pile of rocks and dirt. There was no way over it and no way to tell if the tunnel continued beyond it. He started back, still shining the light on all sides and corners of the cave.

He looked all around the sides of the tunnel very carefully. He didn't want to overlook something obvious and have Bird laugh at him. But there was nothing that looked interesting. It was all just rocks and dirt.

He even looked under rocks and banged hard again with the shovel at the sides of the tunnel. But once when he did that, a shower of dirt came down on his head. Finally, he turned and scrambled back outside, hugely relieved at the feel of fresh air and sunshine on his skin. Cousin had waited for him outside and now danced around him, wagging his tail, also obviously relieved.

Pete sat on a rock and stared at the cave. It was hot and he was sweaty. He felt as if he were covered in mould and dirt and spiderwebs. He went back down through the trees to the cave by the lake. He wanted time to think. He stripped off his clothes and ran naked into the water. He swam and spouted in the clear water like a goofy whale, and then he came back out and sat on the sand. A little wind came up on the lake and the sunlight began to crinkle and dance across the walls of the cave. Pete loved it when this happened. It was like being underwater. He lay there, half asleep, for a long time, while Cousin lay beside him.

Eventually he began to feel hungry. It was getting late. Rob might be at the house looking for him, but he needed to have one more look at the tunnel to make sure he hadn't missed anything. He picked up the shovel and the bag of tools and climbed back up the hill, through the tangled trees, and into the gully to the fallen tree and the mouth of the cave. He stared at it for a while, then sighed heavily. He crawled back inside, had a good look, and then went out again. Nothing. Probably his grandmother already knew about the tunnel, and he was just making an idiot of himself. Again. He should have waited and asked his grandmother. He decided to climb out of the gully over the rocks beside the tunnel. Maybe there was an easier way back through the dark, thick forest.

At the top of the gully, he suddenly stopped. There was a hole at his feet. He stared, trying to make sense of it all. This was roughly the same direction the tunnel took as it went into the hill. Maybe this was where the cave-in had happened. Maybe the tunnel continued past the wall of rock and mud.

He stuck the shovel in the ground at the edge of the hole and began to dig. He dug all around the edges of the hole, trying to widen it out enough so he could see inside. While he worked, he thought about his grandma in the hospital. He thought about his busy parents. He sighed. If his mother did come, she would ask him a million questions about what he had been doing, then she'd find something wrong and insist he go home with her. Just when he was really starting to like it here.

He stabbed the shovel into the ground one more time when suddenly the ground crumbled under him. He reached out, grabbed for a root, got his fingertips on it, but it was too late. The root broke in his hand and then he was sliding down in a shower of stones and dust, down into the narrow tunnel below! He landed with a thump in a patch of mud and rock. The landing jarred the air out of his lungs and for a moment he was curled up on his side, choking, just wanting to breathe. He gasped, coughed, and then began to breathe easier. The air stank of mould and mud. There was a trickle of water coming out of the dirt by his head; it made a small puddle then disappeared under the mound of rocks and dirt that must be what was blocking the tunnel. He gathered his strength until he could sit up, turn over and boost himself to his feet. But when he tried to stand, his ankle crumpled under him; he had to lean on the muddy wall beside him to keep from falling. The pain was so intense that sweat broke out all over his body. He felt sick. He bent over, waiting for it to subside.

He looked around. He couldn't see much but rocks and dirt, but above him Cousin's head poked through the hole. If Pete hadn't been in so much pain, he would have laughed. Cousin managed to look both worried and astonished at what he must have thought was Pete's crazy behaviour.

"Cousin," Pete called. "Get help. Go home, find someone." Cousin just stood there, looking worried. Suddenly he disappeared and Pete hoped, by some miracle, that Cousin had understood him, but a few minutes later, Pete heard him whining on the other side of the rock wall and scratching at the rocks there. Well, he had the right idea but it wasn't going to do Pete much good.

What was he going to do now? He could try climbing but with his ankle feeling the way it did, he probably wouldn't get far. The hole wasn't that high up but it was high enough. He could try yelling but who would hear him? He could just sit down and wait. Sooner or later Fern or Rob or someone would show up and get him out of this stupid mess. Then he'd end up in the hospital beside his grand-mother. His mother would have proof that he could never be trusted to be on his own ever again, and she'd lock him in his room until he was eighty-five. Bird and Jess would have a good laugh. And he hadn't even found any gold.

The bag with the matches and flashlight was still above him, but the shovel had fallen into the hole with him. Well, he'd just have to dig himself out. Somehow. How did you dig yourself out of a hole, he wondered? It was cold and damp and he realized he was shaking. He remembered what Rob had said about shock. He was supposed to stay warm. Yeah, right. Well, he'd get warm when he got out of this mess.

He decided to tackle the wall of dirt and rock that lay be-tween him and the rest of the tunnel. He stuck the shovel into the dirt and heaved. It jammed on something. When he pulled the shovel back, a bone came with it, then a bunch of tiny bones that looked . . . like finger bones.

Pete dropped the shovel and put both hands over his mouth. He stood there, trying not to scream for what seemed like an eternity, and then his brain began to work again. Reluctantly, he dropped to his knees. He reached out one hand and touched one of the tiny bones. It seemed icy cold and he snatched his hand back. He sat back on his heels, staring.

Pete grabbed the shovel and began very carefully to scrape away the dirt around the hand. He uncovered more of the hand, then the arm bone, and finally some ribs. And there, beside the ribs, was something wrapped in layers and layers of rotten cloth.

No wonder Pierre had never showed up. He had been trapped in a cave-in. Was the map he had supposedly gone to fetch wrapped in the cloth?

Gritting his teeth, he slowly dug away the mud and sand until the package was revealed. Then, carefully, he reached toward the flap of rotten cloth. He was afraid he might throw up. But underneath the cloth was something hard and smooth. He pulled it out and carefully unwrapped the rotten, tattered cloth from around it. Inside was a leather pouch. The wooden button that had once fastened it had rotted away. Pete started to lift the flap, hardly daring to breathe, but the leather tore in his hand.

He'd wait until later, he thought. He closed the flap. He'd look at it when he was safe. He stuck it in his waistband under his shirt. The last thing he wanted was to die here, beside Pierre, in a dark damp hole in the ground. In fact, what he wanted more than anything else was to get as far away from here as he could. He could feel himself shaking. He was afraid at any moment he might start screaming and not be able to stop. In fact, maybe that was a good idea.

"Help!" he screamed. "Help, help!" He waited and listened. There was only the silence of the tunnel, the silence of what he now knew was a grave. "Help me!" he screamed again. He started to panic. All he wanted to do was scream, but he stopped himself by shoving both hands in his mouth. His hands tasted of mud. He spat, gagged, almost threw up.

In desperation, he began to slam at the walls with the shovel, pulling down dirt and rocks. Once a rock slammed into his hurt ankle and he yelled with the pain of it. Bright red lights of pain danced behind his eyes. When the pain subsided, he began again, but more carefully. He had to stand on one leg and push the shovel towards the wall. He kept pulling down shovelfuls of dirt and rock and then standing on them. Gradually, he worked his way higher and higher. He had to rest every few minutes. It was taking a long time but it was working. There were several roots dangling from the fallen tree, just over his head. If he could reach those — if they didn't break off — if they were strong enough — maybe he could pull himself up over the edge.

His stomach hurt. He was starving and cold and exhausted. Cornflakes and raspberries weren't enough food to fuel this kind of effort. He kept on digging with a kind of dogged crazy desperation. He wondered what had happened to Cousin. Maybe he had become bored with this silly new human game and gone home. But his grandma had said Cousin could understand English. Maybe he had gone for help.

At last Pete got high enough on the wall where he could just reach the roots dangling down over his head. If they held, he'd have to swing his good leg up onto the bank and then somehow hoist himself. Out. He rehearsed it in his head, just how it could work. Then he reached up, grabbed, swung, grabbed again desperately with his other hand for a bigger stronger root, swung his good leg up, just as he had planned, then with a huge wrench, pulled himself out and safely onto the ground. He lay there gasping, then sat up and looked around. It was late. He wasn't sure how much time had passed but it was now almost completely dark.

Rob would be so choked. He would probably figure Pete was hiding on him so he could stay at the farm by himself.

A bank of rolling black clouds had piled up over the dim distant mountains. He was shivering with cold and with the effort of getting himself out of the hole. He tried but he couldn't seem to stop shaking. Even his teeth were chattering. Amazing, he thought, they really did chatter, just like in the stories he'd read. They actually made a noise.

He felt all over his ankle and decided perhaps it wasn't broken, just sprained. But he had no idea how to really tell. He managed to stand up and even take a few steps, but he realized he wasn't going to be able to walk very far, certainly not up through the woods, over the fallen logs and rocks. How was he going to reach home? He would have to go down the hill, towards the lake. Mostly he wanted to get away from this place. He was terrified that any moment Pierre's ghost was going to appear again.

He hunted around with his hands in the dim forest light until he found what he was looking for — a long, straight stick. He had to hoist himself onto one knee, then painfully haul himself to his feet. He limped very slowly, leaning on the stick. A couple of times he almost fell, and every time he tried to put weight on his leg, the pain made him stop, made him feel sick and sweaty and faint. He would close his eyes until it went away, and then continue. Every time he closed his eyes, he could see the bones again. He kept looking behind him, wanting desperately not to see the white shape of a dead man.

He was so tired. He hadn't realized until now how much pain he was in. His hands hurt where he had scraped them on the rocks when he fell. His back muscles ached from all the digging and his stomach twisted in hunger. When he reached the bottom of the hill, it seemed impossible to him to continue. Carefully, he lowered himself to the ground, with his bad leg sticking out in front of him. I'll just rest a bit, he thought, just rest.

From far away he heard a voice calling his name, and he wanted to open his eyes and respond but it seemed like so much effort. The voice went on calling and calling, but it was so wonderful just to rest, and sleep and not worry about anything.

Then suddenly, he felt himself being shaken, hands were lifting him up, and a blanket was being wrapped around him.

"Pete, Peter, wake up, what happened? Come on, open your eyes, please. Please!" It was Bird's voice.

He opened his eyes and there she was looking down at him, and there was Jess as well, with Rob peering over their shoulders, and of course, there was Cousin, licking his face and dancing around and bouncing in the air like a crazy dog.

"What happened?" Jess demanded. "Man, we've been looking all over for you! When we got to the farm, Cousin was running around, whining and crying like he was trying to tell us something important. We figured you were in trouble or he wouldn't have left you alone."

"C'mon," said Rob, "let's get you up to the house and warmed up. We can figure it all out later."

"My leg hurts," Pete whispered. It seemed like an effort even to talk.

"What happened?" Jess repeated. "Did you fall off a cliff?"

"Sort of," Pete whispered. He closed his eyes. He could hear everyone talking but it seemed too much of an effort to try to understand or respond. Rob picked him up. He could tell it was Rob because of his deep voice. He felt himself being carried up the hill, and then he heard a car door open and he was being lowered into the seat of a car.

"Get in with him and hold him up, Robin," said Rob. Pete felt Bird's arms go around him. Her hair swung across his face.

"It's okay, Dad, I've got him," Bird said. Rob started the vehicle and they moved slowly up the hill. Pete leaned back on the seat and concentrated on breathing. He could smell Bird's skin. She smelled like strawberries and sunshine. He knew he ought to be embarrassed being held by a girl but he was too tired to care.

The vehicle slowed and stopped.

"Okay, young man. Into the house with you. I'm going to check you over and then we're heading straight for the hospital."

"No . . . way," Pete managed to croak. "I'm fine. I just . . . need to rest. I'm . . . not hurt."

"What about your leg?"

"Sprained. It's . . . nothing."

"I'll decide that. Well, let's get you lying down and I'll have a look."

Pete opened his eyes and looked straight into Bird's face. She was leaning over him, staring at him with concern.

"I can walk," he said. "I'm okay." Except his leg burned like fire when he tried to stand on it. Bird got on one side and her father on the other, and Pete managed to hop his way into the house.

Once Rob had helped him lie down on the couch in his grandma's living room, Pete looked up at the anxious faces all hovering over him and managed a grin.

"Hey guys, I'm okay," he said. "Don't look so worried." His voice came out in a croak. He tried to sit up but Rob's big hand pushed him down again.

"Hey, take it easy for a bit. Let's have a look at that leg." Rob felt his leg carefully, then poked and prodded at other parts of Pete, asking if anything hurt.

"I'm fine," Pete protested again. This time when he tried

to sit up, Rob didn't stop him. Pete was a little dizzy, but a few deep breaths helped that.

"I'm going to tape up that ankle," Rob said, "and then you are coming home with us. And no argument and no more nonsense about staying here by yourself. This time you are staying where we can keep an eye on you. No more lies about who is supposed to be here. I don't like being tricked, young man!"

"Okay," Pete said meekly. "Sorry."

Behind Rob's shoulder, Bird grinned and wiggled her eyebrows at Pete. "This should be fun," she said. "I always wanted a brother to tease!"

Chapter Nine

—

"Okay," said Bird. "Talk to us. What happened to you? What were you doing over there at the tunnel all by yourself? Did you find anything?"

It was the next morning when Pete woke up at Bird's house. The night before, he had managed to eat dinner and then he had gone to sleep right after in the guest bedroom as soon as his head hit the pillow. No one had asked him too many questions. But now it was morning and Jess and Bird were both sitting on the end of his bed, staring at him.

"Wow," said Jess, with open admiration. "When we saw you lying there, you looked dead!"

Bird said, "You promised you'd wait for us."

"I know," Pete said guiltily. "I just couldn't wait. I went to that tunnel thing to investigate, but then I fell in this big hole and sprained my ankle. It took me a while to get out. I had to sort of dig my way out. Then my ankle was so sore, I couldn't make it home. That's when you found me."

It was a long speech for him, but he had still left out all the important parts.

"Oh, and I think I saw a ghost. And I also found something."

"What?" Jess and Bird said in unison.

He stood up, hopped across the room to where his clothes were lying on the dresser, and came back. He threw the flat black leather pouch on the bed.

"And I found a skeleton too," he said. "I think it must be Pierre. We have to tell your father, Bird."

They were silent, staring at him. Then Bird said, "You are one amazing guy. You're so quiet but then you do these crazy things."

Pete shifted uncomfortably.

"I haven't opened it yet," he said. "I didn't look inside. I was too scared, trying to get out of that cave-in."

"What cave-in?" they both said again.

"What exactly happened to you?" Bird demanded. "We thought you disappeared down some kind of hole. You came home, ate everything in sight, and then you went to sleep. You didn't say anything. So. Now. There was a cave-in? And a skeleton! And a ghost! Now talk! All of it. Out with it!"

He told them the story of the strange misty figure in the woods, and then the face at the window, of finding the tunnel, the cave-in, the pit in the ground, the ancient bones and finding the pouch. It was a lot of talking. Every time he stopped Bird stared at him and said, sternly, "Keep going."

"It was Pierre's ghost!" Bird exclaimed when he was done. "It's got to be. And he's trying to tell you to find the gold. He wants you to have it. We've got to go back to that mine."

"No, first, your father has to hear about this," Jess argued. "I think when there's bones involved, you gotta call the cops."

"At least, let's look inside that leather thing first," Bird said. "There might be clues. And if the cops come, they'll just take it away as evidence."

"Is that legal?" Jess asked. "Isn't that like, messing with a crime scene or something."

"It's not a crime scene," Pete said. "I think Pierre died when the cave roof fell on him. I think Bird is right. We have to look in the pouch thing."

They all stared at the ancient black pouch lying on the quilt. The leather was tattered and disintegrating. It stunk, faintly, of mud and mould.

"Okay," Bird said. "But we've got to swear to keep it a secret. Just the three of us."

"Right."

Carefully, Pete reached out and picked up the pouch. He peeled back the flap without tearing it, peered inside and then unfolded the other two sides so it lay flat. It was just a flat tattered dirty black piece of old leather. He stared at it for a long while then threw it on the bed.

"Nothing," he said with disgust.

"Nothing?" Bird picked it up and shook it. Bits of mud fell off onto the carpet.

"All that for nothing." Pete sat down on the bed. His ankle burned.

"Except you found Pierre," Jess said.

"Yeah. Maybe. C'mon," Pete said. "Let's go tell your dad. And then I want to call my grandmother. And have breakfast! And a shower."

Bird and Jess had to help Pete as he limped down the stairs. Bird's mom and dad were up, busy making pancakes, omelettes, toast and bacon, putting juice, milk, jam, butter and syrup on the table.

Pete ate until he couldn't hold another bite. Over breakfast, Pete told a shorter version of the same story. Rob shook his head. "You are one lucky young man," he said sternly. "Those old mine tunnels are nothing to fool around with."

After breakfast, Rob phoned the hospital and talked to Pete's grandmother. She was fine and would be home in the afternoon. Fern would pick her up and bring her to the farm.

The police arrived right after that, driving a white police SUV, roaring up the driveway with their lights flashing. They slid to a halt with a crunch and slither of gravel and then banged on the door. Rob went to answer it. He came inside followed by two Mounties in uniform.

"Here is the young man with the story. His name is Peter Eliot," he said, gesturing to Pete.

Both policemen stared at him. Pete stared at the floor, thinking hard. Was he going to get in trouble for something? After all, he had, sort of, lied to Rob and Fern and his parents.

"So, young man, I hear you've been doing some exploring. Care to tell us what you've been up to?" The cop did not sound friendly. He had a gun on his hip and he looked to Pete to be about eight feet tall.

"I found this old kind of tunnel, or pit thing," Pete said. The words felt like they were stuck behind his teeth and tongue and he had to force them out one by one. He was sick of telling this story. Plus, for no reason at all, the police made him feel guilty. Even when he tried, he couldn't look right at the policeman.

"I fell into part of it and when I was trying to get out, I found some, um, bones or something."

"And what did these bones or something look like?"

"Well, it kind of looked like a hand." Pete glanced at Rob who was also looking disapproving.

"Well, you're going to have to show us where this tunnel-pit-something is." The tall cop turned to the other one.

"Probably nothing to it," he said. "Might be a deer or some-thing. But I guess we have to check it out."

The other cop nodded. "Care to tell us what you were doing wandering out in the woods all by yourself? Where are your parents?" he asked.

" My dad's in Russia. My mom's in Victoria."

"Russia?" the big cop said.

"He plays music," Pete mumbled.

"Music." The cop snorted. It sounded as though he thought music was a waste of time.

"So who was looking after you?"

Fortunately, Rob intervened at this point. "He's here on vacation to see his grandmother. She's in the hospital. She fell, just a minor accident. She's okay, coming home today. He was just at the farm to do chores and then he was going to spend the night here. Right, Pete?"

"Right," Pete mumbled.

After that, he got to ride in the back of the police SUV, which wasn't too bad. Rob came behind in his Jeep with Bird and Jess. Once they arrived, the police unloaded climb-ing ropes and rappelling gear, and then they all walked through the woods to the hole in the ground. Pete had to limp slowly on his sore ankle. A couple of times, it hurt so much that he felt himself start to sweat. But he made it. He was still stiff and sore and moving made him feel better.

The hole wasn't as deep as Pete remembered it but when he saw it, he started to shake. He was doing his best to pretend he was okay until Bird came up beside him. Very quietly, she took his hand, and said, "Don't look inside. Let them do it."

Her hand was warm and soft on his and felt like some kind of lifeline, feeding him strength and energy.

The big cop strapped himself into the gear, hitched the rope securely onto a tree, and then lowered himself into the hole on the rope and then climbed back out.

"It's human, all right," he said. "You weren't kidding, son. Well, I'll be darned. We'll have to call in a team from the coast for this one." He shook his head and then looked at Pete as if he were seeing him for the first time. "These old mine shafts are darn dangerous, Pete. Hills around here are full of them. Crazy prospectors thinking they were going to strike it rich. They left holes everywhere. Most of them have been blocked off; otherwise people could get killed in them. You're lucky you're still here and you made it out of this one by yourself. That took guts. And smart thinking. Well, I'll be darned."

He shook his head again and went on his way. Pete wasn't sure if he was supposed to feel complimented or not. He stumbled and limped back out of the woods with Bird and Jess on either side, holding him up, and when they all got back to the farmyard, there was his grandmother, stepping down from Fern's truck and holding out her arms to greet him.

That evening, Pete made the fire in the fireplace all by himself while his grandmother looked on with admiration. Fern had left them a pan of lasagna, and after they ate, he did the dishes without being asked, fed Cousin and the cats, and when the fire was burning, they sat side-by-side staring into the flames.

He told his grandmother parts of the story. In little bits and pieces, he told her about the ghost, about falling in the pit, about the skeleton. She asked questions whenever he stopped and that helped him to talk. He didn't talk about how scared he had been, and he also left out the leather thing. He didn't really care if he ever saw it again. He left out being mad at Jess and Bird, and he left out Bird holding his hand, although he had certainly thought about it, over and over. Each time he did think about it, he got the same strange shivery little thrill.

After he had done talking, they sat silent for a while. Then a log popped and partly exploded in the fireplace.

"Spirits walking," said his grandmother.

Pete looked at her.

"That's what the Indian people say, anyway. Me, I think it's just old moisture trapped in the log."

"Grandma, there's no such thing as spirits. Are there?"

She frowned. "Pete, I don't know, and I don't think anyone really knows. The older I get, the more I think the world is a strange and wonderful place. There's so much we don't know. There might be spirits. There might not. But you don't have to decide, you know. You can just let things be mysterious."

"Was that a real ghost I saw? Do you think it was Pierre's ghost?"

"Well, it was late, it was dark, and you were tired. Hard to say what it was."

"But what about the face in the window?"

"Maybe you were dreaming."

Pete sat back in his chair, trying to remember.

"But everyone sees strange things sometimes," his grandmother went on. "My dad, your grandpa, died the year before you were born. In fact, you were born the next year on his birthday, July 28. After he died, for a while, this farm felt strange. I don't think my father ever wanted to leave. In his later years, he never left the farm at all. I went to town and did all the shopping and chores. I sometimes wonder if the farm and the animals missed him too. I missed him more than I ever thought I would. We fought all our lives. Maybe I missed fighting with him. After my mother died, he got hard and mean and bitter."

"So what did you see?"

"Oh all kinds of strange things. One morning I woke up, and there was a giant grey spotted cat curled up on the bed. When I reached out my hand to it, it flowed down off the bed and disappeared. And another time, when I was sitting down here in the living room, it sounded like all the furniture upstairs was being thrown around. I finally screwed up the courage to go upstairs but I didn't see anything."

"Wow."

They sat in silence a little longer and then his grand-mother yawned and said she was going to bed.

Pete sat by the fire for another half-hour, but nothing spooky happened, no voices or visions. Only the logs in the fire kept popping and exploding, and each time it hap-pened, he jumped in his chair.

The next morning, after breakfast, Pete's grandmother said, "I've been thinking about you looking for these gold coins, Pete. I don't think you're going to find them but I did re-member something you might be interested in. I forgot, but I've got a bunch of Pierre's old letters. They're all in French so I stuffed them away upstairs and forgot about them. There's a bunch of his old books as well. But maybe there's something interesting in the letters."

"I can't read French," Pete said.

"Yes, but Bird can. She was in French immersion before she came here and now she gets French tutoring. C'mon upstairs. They're in the attic somewhere."

He followed up the stairs. She had to stop and breathe heavily when she got to the top, but then she reached up and pulled a handle. A set of stairs came down out of the ceiling.

"They're in a trunk somewhere," she said, as she started up the stairs. "Now let me see, I haven't been up here for years."

Pete followed her into the dusty attic. There were several ancient black wooden trunks along the wall, and a pile of what looked at first like junk.

"Hmm ... which trunk ... ?" she muttered. Pete was looking at the junk. It was mostly old toys: several metal trucks, some plastic action figures, a pile of toy guns, and a metal lunch bucket that when he opened it, was full of Lego.

"Was this my dad's?"

But his grandmother wasn't listening. "Found it," she said triumphantly.

She held up a black leather case.

"C'mon, let's go downstairs. It's too dusty up here."

Pete followed her, although he wanted more time to look at the toys.

Downstairs, she sank heavily into a chair, opened the case and pulled out several sheets of fragile, thin paper with spidery faint blue writing.

"Can't read a thing," she said. "Go call Bird, see if she wants to come over."

But Bird, it turned out, wasn't home and neither was Jess. He left messages for both of them.

"Guess it will have to wait," Pete's grandmother said. "Pete, can I get you to go check on the chickens. Maybe give them a bit of grain, like I showed you. I'm still not feeling that great. I think I'll just lie down for a bit."

And indeed, when Pete looked at her, he realized her face was drawn and thin. She looked very old, suddenly, and he stuck out his hand in case she fell but she laughed, a dry kind of chuckle.

"Oh, I can still stand on my own. I'll be okay. I just need to rest. I'll be back downstairs in a bit."

She went towards the stairs. He stood still until he heard her bedsprings creak overhead and then he and Cousin went outside in the bright morning filled with bird song. He did the chores and then went and sat in the hayloft again. It was quickly becoming his favourite place.

Chapter Ten

—

Bird sat down and unfolded the sheets of crumbling paper carefully across her knees. "It looks like some kind of diary," she mused, and started to read aloud: "March 21, 1921. Last night was most fortunate. I won again. My winnings are piling up. But the men are looking at me with suspicion. I must be careful. I know some of them think I am cheating."

She turned over the sheet of paper, and continued reading: "My family is much on my mind these days. I don't even know if my parents are still alive. Perhaps now that I have the money, I will get up the courage someday to write to them or even go visit. I would like them to know a little of my life here. It is so different from anything I could ever have imagined growing up as a boy. Since coming to Canada, I have been very fortunate. I am now a wealthy man with land, livestock, and a good strong house. If my luck continues, perhaps I will finally be able to marry and have a family to carry on after me."

"What about the gold?" Jess interjected, dancing from foot to foot in his impatience.

"Wait, there's more," Bird said. She continued: "April 21, 1921. I have so many enemies. I have reason to think they might still be after me for my riches. I have talked to William Eliot about this. He is a good man and I think I can trust him. I am going to give him the map I have made."

"William Eliot. That was my grandfather's name. And his father's name too," Pete said.

"I think he must mean your great-great-grandfather," Jess said. "But where was he getting all this gold?"

"Grandma said he liked to play poker," said Pete. "He won it. It sounds like the other miners were jealous."

Carefully, Bird unfolded the rest of the paper.

"There's a lot more diary here," she said, "but no map. I'm going to take this home and finish translating it. I can get my tutor to help. I think this will be fascinating."

Pete took the fragile grey paper from Bird's lap and stared at it.

They were sitting in the cave at the beach. Bird and Jess had arrived on their bikes in the afternoon. Pete and his grandmother had made lunch together and then she sighed. "Sorry, Pete, I'm going to have to lie down again. These old ribs just won't quit aching. I should be back to my old self in a couple of days."

"We might as well go back to the house," said Bird. "Your grandma might be up by now. She'll probably be very interested in this, but I am personally very disappointed. When I got your message, I was quite sure there would be clues. I was sure we would solve this mystery."

Her red hair was braided and the braids swung against her tanned face. Her brown eyes had little golden glints in them that Pete had never noticed before. Her face was very serious. Sometimes, he thought to himself, she talked just like a schoolteacher.

"Yeah, I'd better go do the chores," Pete said.

"So what, you're a farmer now?" Jess said. "Pretty fast for a city boy."

"Grandma showed me what to do. I like it."

"Maybe you're like your grandfather," Bird said. "My father says people are very influenced by genetics, more than they realize."

More schoolteacher, Pete thought. But he only nodded.

They had to walk slowly because of Pete's ankle. When they reached the house, a black Mercedes SUV was sitting in the yard.

"Hey," Pete whispered to Bird and Jess, "that car belongs to the real estate guy. What's he doing here?"

Cousin started to whine and trotted toward the barn.

"He's out at the barn," Jess said. "Come on, let's see what he's up to."

They hurried as fast as they could. Pete's ankle was burning but he gritted his teeth and kept up. As they got closer to the barn, Cousin began to bark, and then he took off at a run.

Up ahead, they heard a man yell. Cousin yipped, a high, hard, hurt sound. Then he started barking again. The man was just outside the main door of the barn; he was swinging a cane, trying to hit Cousin, who was dancing, barking and growling and trying to stay out of the reach. But he was keeping one foot off the ground, dancing on three legs instead of four.

Then the man swung the cane again, a hard vicious swing that smacked Cousin on the side of his head. The little black dog collapsed in the dirt.

"Oh, no, Cousin!" screamed Bird. "He's killed Cousin!" She flew towards the man like a furious eagle. "You leave our dog alone!" she shrieked. The man stopped swinging his cane as Bird grabbed his arm. Jess was right behind her. He grabbed the man's other arm.

The man staggered under their weight. "Get away from me!" he yelled. "You kids are nuts. Leave me alone! Get off me, let go of me!"

Bird and Jess had now managed to topple the man over and Bird was now kicking him hard in the leg. Then suddenly she stopped and ran to Cousin and fell to her knees beside him.

Jess was now standing over the man, holding the cane that the man had dropped. The man's face was red and sweating; he looked so silly sitting there among the cow pies in a business suit and tie. Pete would have laughed if things hadn't been so serious.

"Cousin, Cousin," said Bird. She had Cousin's head in her lap. "He's just knocked out," she said. "He's still breathing. I think he's going to be okay. He'd better be," she glared at the man, "or you're going to be charged with murder."

"You kids are nuts," the man said. Then his voice softened. He mopped at his red face with a handkerchief. "Look, I'm sorry, I didn't mean to hurt your dog. I'm afraid of dogs. I'm afraid of cows too, so when I came out here, I brought that cane. Then the dog attacked me, and when I tried to defend myself, you kids attacked me. And that dog is a vicious animal, he should be on a leash or in a pen."

"And you're a trespasser," said Pete. "That dog has the right to keep trespassers off our property."

"I'm not a trespasser," the man said. "I'm just here doing my job." He managed to sit up. "Ow, lady, you got one mean kick there."

"Well, this farm is my grandma's," Pete said. "And you're the reason why she fell and hit her head. You should go, right now!"

"What?"

"She said you called her names and then she fell and we had to take her to the hospital."

"Whoa, whoa, you kids got the wrong idea here," said the man. "I didn't know any of this. I just came out here to check on a few things. I knocked on the door but no one answered. I wouldn't call your grandma names. I really like that old lady. I'm the one who is trying to help her out. She's one of the most interesting people I know. Real old-timer."

"Check on what?" Bird said. She was still kneeling on the ground with Cousin's head in her lap. Cousin had opened his eyes and was licking her hand with his pink tongue. "Oh, Cousin, you're all right. Oh poor, sweet little dog."

Pete stared at the man. His stomach was doing flip-flops.

The man finally finished levering himself up off the ground. "Whew! Look, can we go somewhere and talk? I think we need to clear a few things up. I'm just here finishing a property assessment, which, by the way, your grandmother asked me to do. So now, if you kids are done assaulting and harassing an ordinary citizen, I need something to drink and somewhere to wash." He looked distastefully at his dusty hands. There was cow manure on his pants and shoes.

He limped towards the house, dusting off his clothes and swearing under his breath. The other three looked at each other.

"Okay, I'm confused," Jess said. "What's a property assessment? And why did your grandmother ask him to do one?"

"I'm not sure," Bird said, "but doesn't it have something to do with selling?"

"Let's get back to the house," Pete said. "I don't trust that man no matter what he says."

"Cousin," Bird said, "you're such a good, good dog." Cousin wagged his tail. He got to his feet and then trotted off to the cow's water trough and had a long drink of water. He came back and licked Pete's hand. They all took turns petting him and telling him he was a good dog.

"Do you really think Grandma has decided to sell the farm?"

"Well, let's go find out," Bird said. "You need to ask her straight out. Don't be a wuss."

A wuss! How dare she call him that, after he had dug himself out of that tunnel?

"I'm not," he said.

"I thought you loved this place," she said. "I thought you loved your grandma. You know she would probably agree to sell only because she thinks she has to because she doesn't have any money, and she thinks no one else cares. She'll die of grief if she has to leave this place. So don't let her. Come on, hurry. What is wrong with you?"

"Nothing is wrong with me," he said, limping along with gritted teeth. "What's wrong with you? All you ever do is yell at people. I thought we were friends."

"We are friends. That's why I yell at you. If I didn't care about you, if I didn't really like you, I would just ignore you and walk away and never talk to you again. Get it?"

They glared at each other, and then something inside Pete turned over and fell into place.

"You . . . like me?"

"Oh jeez," she said impatiently. "Don't get all emotional on me. Come on."

They set off back to the house with Cousin at a run.

"I bet that means your grandma is awake," said Jess.

When they straggled in the back door of the farmhouse, Pete's grandmother was sitting at the kitchen table, a cup of tea in front of her, the cat curled up in her lap. The man was sitting next to her, also drinking tea. His face wasn't so red and his hair was combed.

"Pete!" she said. "And Bird and Jess! It's so good to see you. Come and sit down. Pete, you are white as a ghost. That leg is hurting a lot more than you're letting on. Sit down right now, before you fall down. You are supposed to stay off that leg. Rob told me to see to it."

Pete eased himself gratefully into a chair and Bird and Jess took chairs beside him. But he was too upset to relax.

"Grandma — "

"Peter — " she said at the same time.

They both stopped and stared at each other.

"Grandma," Pete said all in a rush, "please don't sell the farm, please."

"Whoa," said his grandma. "What makes you think I'm selling the farm?"

"Well, what's he doing here?" Pete glared at the man.

"Oh, Peter, wait a minute. Let's all calm down. Peter, meet Ed Paterson. Ed, this is my grandson, Pete, and his friends, Bird and Jess. Ed, I think you and Pete met once before. Peter, Ed is doing an assessment for me, to tell me what the place is worth. You know I've been pretty worried about money. And I've been thinking. Maybe the place is getting to be too much, and if your father is never going to want to live here or even come and visit, what's the point of me hanging on so hard? I had a lot of time to think in that hospital. Maybe I'm too old to live here. If I were closer to the city, maybe I could see you a bit more often."

His grandma looked at Pete. "And by the way," she said, "you didn't tell me the whole story either last night. Rob told me you could have died. You kind of skipped that part. So, what's been going on, Pete?"

Pete looked at the floor. He really had to be careful. If she told his mother, his mother would come roaring back all the way from Africa, take him away and ground him for the rest of his life. "I told you, I just sprained my ankle when I fell in this kind of hole thing. It wasn't really dangerous or anything."

"Humph!" said his grandmother. "I think I know when I'm being conned. Oh well, we'll let that version go for now. I'll talk to you more about it later." She turned back to Ed. "I guess I have to apologize for these wild kids. But they thought they were protecting me."

"Avery, I'm sorry. I didn't know you were hurt. Your grandson seems to think it was all my fault."

"Well, you said I was foolish not to at least consider that offer you told me about, and I was mad, and then I went upstairs and fell and hit my head. It wasn't really your fault. I was just upset. I can't stand the idea of my life changing, and you seemed to think it was so simple."

"Avery, I don't know what to say. But I still think a couple of million dollars is a lot to turn down. You know the bank won't wait forever."

"Don't start in on me again. I'm not ready," Pete's grandmother snapped. She put her head in her hands. "I'll talk to you when I'm ready. Not before. Please, just leave me alone. I really hate to be pushed around."

"All right, Avery, it's your call." Ed stood up. "But I'm not the bad guy here. I'm sorry again, but I'm just trying to do the right thing here for everyone. I'll call and check in with you next week when I have the final figures for the assessment."

The kitchen was dead silent when he left.

Then Pete's grandma said softly, "Pete, I really, really need to talk to your dad. Maybe it is time to change my life. Maybe it is time I faced reality."

Pete stood up. He could feel words bubbling around inside him like lava inside a volcano. He could feel the pressure building up inside his head until he felt like a balloon getting bigger and bigger, ready to explode.

"I thought you loved it here." The words came out far louder than he intended.

"Pete, it's not simple," his grandma said. Her eyes filled with tears and she blinked them away. "I'll talk to you later. Right now, I'm going back to bed. You kids enjoy yourselves. Have some ice cream and raspberries."

Pete stood up, turned and went out the back door. He limped down the stairs, hobbled out the back door and across the yard. He heard Bird calling him but he didn't turn around. Cousin bounded and leapt beside him, but Pete ignored him.

"Cousin, get lost," he snapped. "Stay home!" The words were cruel; he knew it and didn't care. Cousin stopped as if he had been kicked. He stared after Pete with a puzzled hurt look in his eyes and walked away with his head down.

Pete limped out to the barn and crawled up the ladder. His face was burning. His throat hurt. He sat down with his back against the hay bales. He didn't feel as if he understood anything anymore. There was just so much to think about, his parents, his grandmother, Bird saying she liked him, the farm, the hideous scary feeling he still got in his stomach when he thought about that mine pit, ghost faces at the window. It was all too much. He didn't want to talk to anyone right now, about anything. Maybe he'd just go to sleep.

He heard Jess and Bird calling him but he didn't answer. After a while, the Jeep Cherokee pulled into the yard and a bit later, it pulled out again.

He came in when it grew dark and a wind came up that

was colder than he could stand. His grandma was nowhere around. There was a plate and silverware on the table, a sandwich, some cookies and juice. He ignored it and went to his room, and then after he lay down, his stomach jumped at him. He went back out to the kitchen and ate the food, hastily, spilling crumbs on his shirt and not caring. Then he piled his plate and silverware in the sink and went back to his room.

He lay on his back on the worn quilt, staring at the ceiling. He had slipped the old leather pouch into his pocket yesterday, just before he got into the police SUV. He stood up, turned on the light, limped to his dresser, got the mouldy ancient pouch and carried it back to his bed. He stared hard at it and then held it up right under the light. Now that the leather had started to dry out, he could see there were actually marks on it.

He stared and stared, turned it around, looked on both sides. The more he looked at the leather, the more it reminded him of something. He turned it upside down, then sideways. That shape, where had he seen it before? Then it felt like his eyes focused and he saw what he was looking at, a very crudely drawn map of the lake. It took some more examination to really be sure. He even got out the atlas and checked the shape, just to be sure. But there were strange markings around the edges of the leather, what looked like a line of stick men and a couple of weird looking circles, or maybe they were suns.

Pierre wouldn't have made this map unless it meant something important, would he? His grandma had said he was crazy. Maybe he was just paranoid. Pierre wanted to be able to share the gold with his family. So why hide the map in the cave? Or perhaps Pierre had been carrying it with him when he died. Or maybe it had been in the cave and when Pierre went to fetch it, he died in the cave-in.

He stared at the map again. His grandma had said that his great-grandfather had stayed overnight with Pierre. Maybe he had slept in this very same room. And then when he came back for another visit, Pierre had disappeared. He had died in the tunnel. Pierre was afraid of something. He said so in the letter. Was someone really after him or was he just crazy?

Pete lay back down and stared at the ceiling while thoughts kept chasing themselves around and around in his head like angry wasps.

Chapter Eleven

—

Pete was sound asleep but something was after him. Something had grabbed his arm and was pulling him towards the dark mouth of the tunnel. It was hard to breathe. He took a deep breath and woke up, gasping.

Cousin had his teeth in the blankets and was yanking at them, growling and shaking his head.

"Cousin," Peter gasped, "let go, what are you doing?"

Cousin stopped growling and dragging on the blankets and stood back, his tail wagging. Then he turned and headed for the door. He stood there but when Pete didn't move, he came back, stood beside the bed, crouching, his yellow eyes fixed on Pete's face.

"What do you want?" Pete rubbed sleep out of his eyes. He looked at his window. It was still dark. Cousin ran to the door and back again; this time, he grabbed Pete's leg in his teeth and pulled.

"Ow, Cousin, have you gone crazy?" Cousin let go and crouched on the floor. But he still stared at Pete. He looked like he was trying to talk.

Pete swung his legs over the side of the bed, yawning. Cousin leapt up and ran out of the room. Pete heard his feet scrabbling up the stairs to his grandmother's room, and then Cousin galloped back down and into Pete's room.

"Grandma?" Pete said. "Is it Grandma?"

Now he was moving, fast, out of his room, down the hall and up the stairs. His grandmother was lying on the rug beside her bed. She was wearing a nightgown and her grey hair was spread out around her.

"Grandma?" Pete dropped to his knees.

She was breathing but she didn't respond to his voice.

He sat back on his heels. Fear shot through his body. What could he do? It was the middle of the night. How could he get help? He remembered Rob's voice. "When someone is hurt, keep them warm."

He pulled a blanket off the bed, covered her with it and wedged a pillow under her head. Then he ran to the phone. Rob had given him a cellphone number on a piece of paper. Where had he left it? His head spun. He couldn't think. Right, in his jeans pocket. He flew downstairs, found his jeans on the floor and fished feverishly through the pockets.

Okay, there it was. He charged back upstairs, grabbed the phone. He misdialed the number twice before he made himself slow down and punch each number carefully.

The phone buzzed in his ear, once, twice, three times, four times. C'mon, he said to himself. Please, please answer.

"Hello," said a sleepy voice.

"It's Pete," he said. "Grandma's on the floor and she won't wake up."

"I'll be right there!" Rob's voice snapped in his ear and the phone clicked.

Pete sat on the floor beside his grandmother, waiting for Rob. Cousin sat beside him. Cousin licked Pete's face and then lay down his with head on Grandma's shoulder.

Pete stared at her. For the first time, it hit home to him that not only was his grandmother old, but that old people died.

He picked up her thin hand. "Don't die, Grandma. Please, please, please, please." The house suddenly seemed terribly quiet and lonely. There was only the sound of his grandma's breathing and his own thumping heart. He stared at her hand. It was brown and wrinkled. Blue veins showed through the skin. It seemed pretty scary, getting old. And his grandma was here by herself. What would have happened to her if he hadn't been here?

After what seemed like hours, Pete heard a car in the yard and then Rob came bounding up the stairs.

"The ambulance is coming," he said. "I was worried

about this. I knew her heart wasn't that strong."

He got busy with his stethoscope and blood pressure cuff. Peter could hear an ambulance siren coming closer and closer. It wailed into the yard and suddenly the house seemed to be full of lights, people and noise. Two men in white coats lifted his grandmother carefully onto a stretcher, carried her downstairs, and slid her stretcher smoothly into the back of the ambulance.

Rob grabbed Pete's arm when he started to follow.

"No way," he said. "You are coming with me, young man. Last time I left you alone, look what happened. You can ride to the hospital with me and then you are staying where I can keep an eye on you. Go get some clothes on."

Pete pulled on his jeans and a t-shirt and then climbed into Rob's vehicle. All the long way to the hospital, he stared miserably out the window. When they reached the hospital, he had to sit by himself in the cold waiting room. This time no one came to rescue him. It was still dark outside. His eyes drooped and he kept yawning.

Finally, Rob came through the door.

"Your grandma has had a heart attack. She's asleep now. She is going to be okay, but she's going to have to take it easy for quite a while. C'mon, I'll take you home."

Back at Bird's house, Pete crawled into the guest bed and fell instantly asleep.

In the morning, he rode back to the hospital with Rob and tiptoed into his grandmother's room.

"I'm okay, sweetheart," she said, as soon as she saw his worried face. "You saved my life, you know. You are a real hero."

"Cousin did it," Pete said. "He came and got me."

"So, you are both heroes."

Pete shrugged uncomfortably.

"I'll be fine," his grandmother insisted. "I'll be home before you know it. But I'm so glad you were there with me."

"But now my mom will totally make me go back to Victoria," Pete said.

His grandmother sighed. "Yes, she probably will."

"I want to stay here. With you. I could help you look after things. I could look after you. And then you wouldn't have to sell the farm."

"Peter, you have school and your friends and your parents. Those things are important too." She sighed deeply. "Pete, I have got myself in a jam. You see, when Jess's dad was dying . . ."

Rob came back in the room and she stopped talking.

"That's enough, young man. Your grandma needs to rest. You can come see her again tomorrow."

Rob took him back to his house. Pete asked about the animals and chores at his grandmother's, and Rob said he and Fern would take care of them. Pete spent the rest of the afternoon moodily playing StarQuest by himself while Bird practised the piano.

After supper, Jess came over and they all played Monopoly. Pete lost and went to bed early.

He woke in the middle of the night. The moon was shining in his window. It was incredibly bright. He sat up in bed and stared out the window. He was still thinking about the map, about Pierre's death, about ghosts and lost gold. The map was so vivid in his head. It was a map of the lake, that much he could tell. But what were those odd hieroglyphic scribbles that looked like stick men and circles?

He had to take another look at the map. He had an idea.

He pulled on his clothes, tiptoed out of the room, carrying his shoes. He eased open the front door and hurried, limping to where the bikes were all stored together, under the carport. He would have to borrow Bird's bike. His ankle still hurt but he would just have to ignore it. He hoped Bird wouldn't be too mad once she realized that what he was doing was important.

He pedalled as fast as he could go, down the long silent moonlit road to his grandmother's house. Along the way, he watched nervously for ghosts, bears, bats, deer, but the road was quiet and empty.

When he curved into the yard, Cousin came running to meet him. Pete hurried into the house, turning on lights as he went. The map lay where he had left it, on the dresser. He picked it up and carried it to the kitchen table, then ran upstairs to his grandmother's room and got the book of Indian pictographs. He flipped through it. Yes, his hunch had been right; there they were, the same drawings. But the map in the book showed him they were across the lake. Why would Pierre haul his gold across the lake? What was over there? An old abandoned town, and the remains of several mines. Plus the railway track!

If Pierre wanted to send something on the train, or sell his fruit and vegetables, his grandma had told Pete, he rowed his boat across the lake. To Silver City. Where the miners were. And their poker games. And their mines . . . their mines from which they had taken a fortune in both gold and silver. Pierre played poker with the miners and got drunk and rowed home in the dark across the black lake water. So he had hidden his gold across the lake. But where?

He stared at the map again. It was too faded to see everything. He carried it to the kitchen and held it up to the light. Very faintly now, he could see marks that looked like a railway track and above the track, a series of black dots. One of them had an X over it.

If he was right about all this, then the gold was hidden across the lake in one of the old mines. He stared out the window at the dark night. The sensible thing, and the right thing to do, would be to go back to Bird's house, wait for morning, and convince everyone that he was right. Then there would be more fussing while everyone got an expedition organized. By then his parents would probably have arrived, and his mother would drag him back to Victoria and he would never even get to hear what happened.

Or he could go now, by himself. Everyone would be so totally mad at him . . . until he appeared with the gold. But he would be careful. He would take supplies, and the right equipment. He rummaged around and found a flashlight, a blanket, some bread and cookies, a bottle of juice, some matches and an old jackknife.

When he reached the beach, he took hold of the rowboat and shoved it into the water. Cousin leapt in. Pete grabbed the oars and rowed out of the bay. It felt good to take all the anger and energy and adrenaline that were in him and use it to make the boat fly through the water. He rowed straight out.

The sky above him was black velvet and glowing with stars. The lake water was also black, except for the small curls of froth behind the boat that caught the starlight and glittered like tiny eyes. The rowing kept his worried thoughts away, so he kept going as hard as he could. He had never been this far out in the lake before. He knew there were no houses on the other side of the lake, just the railway track. But his grandma had said that the big beach in the notch between the two mountains was also the site of the ghost town of Silver City. The book said the Indian paintings were on a flat granite cliff just above that beach. It had to be the place. It had to be what those weird figures on Pierre's map of the lake meant.

Finally, when he was far out in the middle of the lake, he had to stop and rest. The lights of the houses on the shore behind him were tiny now. He had never stopped to realize just how huge the lake was. How deep was it? Suddenly he thought of all the layers of black water under the boat. His heart thumped. What was down there? His grandmother had said the lake never gave back bodies if someone drowned. The water was too cold, she said. The bodies just sank to the bottom. Or maybe the lake monster ate them.

Suddenly, he jumped. He stared into the blackness. He thought he could see something moving on the lake. It was hard to see but there it was again, a wave, curled and crested with white, travelling through the middle of the calm water. He kept staring but that was all he saw. He picked up the oars and began rowing again as fast as he could.

Before he had gone very far, he saw something move in the bottom of the boat. Once again, he jumped. He couldn't help it. Then he held his breath and sat very still. There it was again. It moved into the reflection from the starlight and now he could see that it was a tiny green frog. It moved very slowly and deliberately towards him, came to his foot, crawled slowly and determinedly up his leg, onto his shirt, up his shirt, and onto his shoulder. Then it sat there. Very gently and slowly, Pete turned his head. The frog just sat there. Its eyes shone gold and black in the starlight. Pete put out a finger and touched the frog's back. Its skin felt cool and dry, not slimy.

"What do you want, little frog?" he asked. Pete leaned his head back, staring at the sky. A shooting star blazed for a moment and disappeared. He wanted to make a wish but he couldn't think what to wish for. The whole night felt full of magic and mystery. Maybe Pierre had sent the frog as a sign he was on the right track.

Slowly, he began to row again. The frog stayed on his shoulder. It took a long time but gradually the other side of the lake came closer and closer. The mountains seemed much steeper here. Finally, just as the sky was beginning to turn pearly grey, the prow of the rowboat grounded on the sand.

Pete stood up and Cousin jumped out on the sand. The frog had disappeared somewhere. He had never been so tired and stiff. Before he did anything else, he had to have five minutes of sleep. He pulled the boat up on the sand and then staggered up the beach towards a row of trees. The sand was soft under the trees, and he curled up with his head on his arms. Cousin curled up next to him. Pete was chilled but Cousin's warmth was comforting. Gradually, his muscles relaxed; he let go of the tension from rowing and slid into a dark pool of sleep.

Then he was swimming in the water, the deep, jet-black water that went on forever. A scaly green body came up beneath him and he was flying over the water. The frog was sitting on his shoulder; the body beneath him went faster and faster. Suddenly it slid again beneath the water and began to take him down with it. He started to panic and choke as the water rushed down his throat . . . and then, abruptly, he woke on the grey, lonely beach, shivering in the dawn light. He lay still, confused by the transition from the strange dream to this stranger reality.

After a few moments, he rolled over on the sand, his whole body stiff and sore, especially his shoulders. Groggily, he sat up and looked around. The beach was grey; the sun hadn't come up yet. A creek was running near by. Above him was a mountain full of silent trees. Cousin came over and licked his face, then grabbed a stick and tossed it up in the air, prancing and wiggling his whole body.

Pete picked up the stick and threw it in the air, and Cousin leapt after it. Pete flopped back down on the ground. It was so quiet. He couldn't remember the last time in his life he had felt so alone. He tried to think about last night, the long row across the black flat water. The frog!

He jumped up and raced down to the boat. At first there was no sign of the frog, but then Pete saw it, sitting calmly on the bottom of the boat in a small pool of water.

"Smart frog," he said. He put his finger down but the frog ignored him. In the light, it was only a small green frog with gold and black eyes. Pete left it sitting there, and pulled the plastic-wrapped map out of his knapsack. He studied it again. If he was right, there should be some Indian hieroglyphics near this beach. He hurried up over the sand to the line of rocks at the edge of the beach. Yes, there they were, a couple of red figures with what looked like many-rayed suns over their heads. He was definitely on the right track!

But the map showed more pictographs, farther up the mountain. He'd have to look for them. And, he'd have to hurry.

By now Rob might already have discovered he was missing, and he would be freaking out and calling Pete's parents. But if he hurried, maybe he could get back before anything really crazy happened. Like his parents calling the cops. He hadn't really thought this out before he left. He'd just had an idea and he'd gone with it. Now, with the day coming, it was beginning to seem both a lonely and foolish thing to do. Why hadn't he waited?

Hunger grabbed him along with loneliness. He pulled out the cookies and juice and devoured them. But they seemed barely to touch the hunger inside him; in fact, they just made him hungrier.

He looked at the boat. All he had to do was jump in and start rowing. In a couple of hours, he'd be home. Everyone would be mad at him but when his parents finally arrived, he could pack up his stuff, get in the car and go back home to his old life. At least his friends would be glad to see him. He could dive back into his computer, back into his favourite video games, back to the familiar routine of school and hanging out and being bored. He'd probably never see the farm or his grandmother again, though. And that was something he didn't want to think about. So now that he was here, he had better get on with whatever it was he had come to do.

He whistled to Cousin, and then walked up through the woods, up the rocky embankment, and onto the railway tracks that stretched away along the base of the mountain. They shone like silver in the dawn light.

He stared around him. Not far away, a creek ran down the mountain, burbling over rocks and sand. What had his grandma said, that the creek ran down beside the main street of Silver City? Okay, then he would follow the creek.

He clambered down the other bank of the railway track and began to push his way through the thick brush beside the creek. The brush quickly gave way to enormous cedar trees with clear space under their sweeping branches. When he got through the cedar trees, he stopped and held his breath. He was on what must have been the main street of the town. On either side of what looked like it had once been a road were the remnants of walls, piles of boards covered with vines and brush, even the remains of log walls crumbling under moss. He could see where the houses must have been, even though there were trees and brush growing over everything. He stopped when something clinked under his foot. He picked up a length of very rusty chain, examined it, and threw it down again.

He walked very slowly. Cousin followed at his heels with his head down. What a weird place, he thought. A wagon wheel lay on the moss with small trees growing through it. He passed some rotting remains of what looked like school desks and then some church pews. When he looked more closely, he could see that, even under the large trees, there were other remains of fallen-down buildings. It must have been big. A ghost city, his grandma had called it.

As he went higher up the mountain, the remains of the old buildings started to disappear, but the road continued, only it began to narrow to just a path between bushes and rocks. Gradually, as he climbed higher, he entered a narrow valley, and soon he was following a path that wound alongside a high cliff of polished-looking stone. He had to stop to climb over a pile of rocks, and when he looked at the cliff, he understood. The mines. There was a hole in the cliff above the pile and just past that hole, another.

Was one of them where Pierre had hidden the gold? Where were the rock paintings?

Then, around a corner, he saw them, a series of stick men, painted high up on the flat face of a granite cliff beside two round red suns. He stared. There was the sign but now what?

He looked at the map again. There it was, a black circle beside the stick men. That must be the old mine tunnel.

He looked up. There was a dark shadow higher up on the cliff. Now he could see there was a sloping ledge on which it should be possible for him to climb. There was a crack just above the ledge with what looked like rocks wedged into it to serve as handholds. He'd practised climbing on the artificial wall at the local sports store with his friends. This didn't look that hard. In fact, it looked like a kind of ladder.

Pete began climbing. He pulled himself from rock to rock. The sun came up over the mountains on the other side of the lake, and slick yellow light began layering over the granite rock and the blue-green dancing, frothing water in the creek.

Everybody would be awake by now. They'd know he had gone. They'd probably head straight for the farm and discover the rowboat was gone. How long would it be before they came looking for him?

As the sun hit him, so did the heat. At first it was welcome, then he felt it begin to burn along his back and legs. His ankle ached and burned. He stretched up his arms, fished with his one good leg for a secure place to put his foot, and then finally pulled himself over the top and onto the ledge in front of the mine.

He fished his flashlight out of his pack. Cousin had followed him up, picking his way delicately along the crack in the rocks. Should he take Cousin inside or should he make him stay outside in case he needed help?

"Cousin, wait here," he said. Cousin gave him a disgusted look and sat down, then curled up with his head on his paws.

This tunnel was very different from the muddy hole above the beach at his grandma's farm. There were big square pieces of wood standing up at intervals along the tunnel, with a thick square plank going across them under the roof of the tunnel. He could walk upright, no crawling this time. The tunnel was dry but dusty.

He flashed his light at everything but nothing looked like

gold or even something that could contain gold. He kept going, farther and farther, until the light from the tunnel mouth was just a round tiny beam, like a distant eye. He started to feel really freaky. He must be deep under the mountain. How far did this mine go? He came to a place where the tunnel branched. Which way to go? He hesitated. Fear stabbed at him. It was hard to breathe. He started to gasp for air. Out, he had to get out.

But as he turned to leave, he hesitated. Where could you hide something in a mine like this? There were only the rock walls and the wooden beams. But wait, he thought, flashing the light above him, the roof wasn't even. There was space above the beams. He started to go back out very slowly, feeling above the beams, and just as he neared the entrance, about ten metres in from the opening, he felt something strange with his fingertips, something that felt like a box, sitting on top of the beam.

He pulled himself up with his hands so he could peer over the beam. It was a box! He tried to move it but it was very heavy and he was too short. He could barely budge it. He needed something to stand on. He dashed for the entrance, looked around. An old, rotten piece of squared wood lay just outside the tunnel mouth. He dragged it back inside. When he stood on it, he could just get his hands on the box. It took all his strength to lever the box off the slab of wood and, even then, he almost dropped it. He lowered it to the ground.

There was something inside it that looked like cloth. He

grabbed it and pulled. It was an ancient woven sack that tore easily, and inside the sack, was a leather sack with a string tying it closed, and when he finally, with shaking fingers, undid that, he saw that inside the sack was a pile of gold and silver coins.

Pete fell on his knees. He'd done it. Wait until his grandmother and Bird and Jess saw this. And his parents. They'd never call him useless again.

He pulled one of the coins out and looked at it, but in the dim light from the tunnel entrance he couldn't really see it. He stood up and half carried, half dragged the sack to the tunnel entrance. The bag of coins was incredibly heavy. He sat in the sun, with his sore leg stretched out in front of him, and began pulling coins one by one, out of the sack, staring at them, letting them drop back inside. He ran his hands through the coins, letting them slide, cool and thin, through his fingers. Was this real or was he still dreaming? It was too hard to take it all in.

It was very hot in the sun. Finally, he stuffed the sack of coins into his backpack, hoisted it onto his back and then stepped over to the edge of the cliff. He still wanted to look at them but that would have to wait for later. When he thought of showing them to his grandmother and to Bird and Jess, he could hardly breathe for excitement.

He clambered carefully back down the cliff, and then hurried under the trees, through the brush, over the railroad track, and onto the stretch of white sand beach. And stopped.

Down at the edge of the beach, where he had left the boat pulled up on the sand was only dark green water. A wind had come up and waves were crashing on the beach. He looked up and down the lake. There was the boat, drifting farther and farther away. As he watched, the wind caught it, spun it around, sent it dancing and gliding over the ruffled surface of the water.

He stood there with his mouth open for several minutes. He hadn't pulled the boat up far enough and the waves had pulled it off the sand. It was totally his fault. No one to blame but his own dumb self. He looked at Cousin as if the dog might have an answer. But Cousin just looked back at him, a puzzled expression on his face. He looked from Pete to the boat as if to say, You're the human. Do something.

"Arrgh!" Pete yelled. But all the yelling in the world wouldn't get the boat back. And the wind was pushing it away faster than he could swim.

Okay, fine, he and Cousin would walk home. He knew what he had to do. He had to walk south, along the railway tracks, to where the train trestle crossed the river at the south end of the lake. He didn't know how far it was, and he sure didn't want to keep walking on his sore ankle with the heavy backpack, but he didn't have a choice. He turned and worked his way through the brush back up towards the tracks, fighting the lashing branches, crawling, scrambling, under, over, and finally there, again, was the railway track, silent and shimmering under the sun.

He heard a strange chopping sound and looked up. A

helicopter was coming along the far southern edge of the lake, flying low, hovering over the edge where the mountains slid into the water. As soon as whoever was in the chopper saw the boat, it veered sharply away from the mountains and out into the lake, hovering over the boat.

Frantically, he waved his arms but the helicopter was too far away and he was behind a fringe of trees.

At least they were searching for him. Then it hit him. Now that they had seen the empty boat, they would think he was dead, drowned in the lake. His parents, his grandma, his friends would all think he had died. He waved again, but the helicopter rose in the air and took off back towards the south. Pete started to panic. He started running and limping down the railway track in the same direction as the helicopter. Then after a few minutes, he stopped, bent over, puffing and heaving for air. Too late. He had to think. He had to get himself out of this mess by himself.

When he reached home, even after he had shown them the gold, he'd still probably have to apologize to everyone and listen to some long boring speech from his parents about responsibility. His mother would be so mad she'd probably ground him for a month. No, for the rest of his life. No TV, no video games. She'd probably never let him out of the house again. Or maybe she'd be so glad to see him and so proud of him, she'd forget all about punishment. Yeah, fat chance. Well, so what? He'd done it, no matter what anyone thought.

Once again, he began walking south along the tracks, limping slowly along in the heat. He was really hungry now. He started thinking about food. As soon as he made it home, no matter what happened or what anyone said, he'd eat everything he could think of — maybe have pancakes or pizza and then some raspberries and ice cream, or maybe he'd have fried chicken and hamburgers and lots of milk or maybe some lemonade.

After half an hour, he and Cousin came to a huge hole in the side of the mountain. Oh no, another tunnel! No more tunnels after this, he thought, not for the rest of his life. He'd never even put his head under the blankets. Never again! He stopped right at the edge and peered in. It was absolutely black inside the tunnel; he couldn't see the other end.

He went in a little ways then stopped again. It was hard to breathe. He went back out and sat down on the hot railways tracks. Cousin leaned against him. The track burned his bum and he slid onto the dusty ground. What if a train came along? He couldn't even see the sides of the tunnel, couldn't see if there was room to get off the tracks. It was very hot. His whole body wanted food and water. The question was, did he want food and water more than he wanted to be sitting here, outside the black tunnel, safe in the sun?

"Cousin!" Pete said. "Cousin, what should we do?" Cousin licked his face and then trotted into the tunnel. He obviously wanted to go home.

Pete felt a small flicker of courage. Cousin knew it was safe. He got up and started forward again. "Cousin . . . ," he continued, talking just to hear his own voice.

"Grandma says you can understand what I say. So what I am saying is, you go ahead and I'll follow you. We've got to get through this somehow. We've got to get home. Okay, I've been an idiot, a total dweeb. I admit it. I should have tied up the boat. I should have checked on it."

The whole time he was talking, he was walking forward. Even with the flashlight on, the darkness surrounded him like soft dust. It penetrated every part of him. He felt like he was vanishing into it. If he turned around, he could see, far away, like a round white dot, the entrance to the tunnel. Then he must have turned a corner or something because even that disappeared. He opened his mouth and panted the way Cousin did when he was too hot. He went on and on through the soft blackness, while Cousin's feet pattered alongside him. He kept flashing the light at the walls but there was nothing to see except rock and more rock. Finally, far ahead, he saw another white dot, the exit to the tunnel. When he finally made it out, he almost collapsed with relief. He took deep breaths of air. But he couldn't afford much time to rest. It was getting late and he wanted to cross the bridge before it was dark.

He hurried along the tracks as fast as he could, limping but trying to ignore his burning ankle and the heavy back-pack, stumbling over the rough broken rock in between the rails. In a couple of hours, when he finally reached the bridge, he didn't stop, just hurried out onto the narrow trestle, stepping carefully on the black railroad ties. Between each wooden tie, he could see the black-green river rolling below him. The bridge crossed the river at a narrow place just before the river surged into the lake. A flock of ducks flew over, their wings whistling as they beat the air. An eagle took off from a tree on the other side of the bridge and circled over him. Every time he looked down, he felt dizzy. He had to stop, take a deep breath, and then focus ahead at the end of the bridge.

Just as he made it to the end of the bridge, he saw another helicopter but this one was far away, circling again over the lake. Could anything more happen to make him feel even worse?

If he had just gone back to the beach, maybe they would have seen him. He would be home by now, fed and safe. He tried waving his arms and yelling again but he was too far away. All he could do was go on.

His feet hurt, his back hurt, his head hurt, his ankle burned, and he was incredibly thirsty, but the river was now far away. His legs felt like lumps of cold, dead metal, except where his feet were rubbed and sore. He realized he no longer felt hungry, but he was dizzy. The pack was far too heavy. It felt like the weight was going to buckle his dead legs. He stumbled over a rock and almost fell. Surely he would be coming to the highway soon. He felt as though he had been walking forever.

Finally, he came to a gate beside the track and he heard

the swoosh of a car far above him. That's where the road was. All he had to do was get himself up there, stick out his thumb and soon he would be safely home. It took all his remaining strength to climb over the gate and drag his weary feet up the narrow dirt road to the highway.

He had been looking forward to the road for so long that when he was finally standing there in the dusk, with a cold wind blowing down off the mountain, it took him a moment to realize he still wasn't home. He began to walk along the highway and, as he walked, he began singing to Cousin, to the trees, to the dark mountains. He couldn't sing very well and his voice sounded funny, even to himself, but it was better than the dark and lonesome silence. He was singing so loud he almost didn't hear the car coming behind him until it stopped and a gruff voice called, "Hey, kid, you need a ride?"

He slung the bulky backpack onto the floor and fell into the car seat. Cousin crawled in beside him. In a voice hoarse with thirst and exhaustion, he whispered, "Can you take me to the hospital, please. I have to see my grandma."

Chapter Twelve

—

Pete stood at the edge of his grandma's yard. It was late evening. His mother's car had just come in the yard while he was out feeding the chickens and doing the rest of the chores.

He watched while both his parents stepped out of the car, stretching and looking around. Despite the fact that they must have both been travelling for days, both were immaculately dressed. His mom's blond hair was tightly curled and she was wearing bright red high-heeled shoes and a long grey skirt. His tall, dark-haired father was wearing a grey suit and a tie. They gathered up their luggage and coats, and then hurried to the door. When his grandmother opened it, they disappeared inside. Pete's throat clenched. He wanted to run to them and put his arms around them. But he stayed in the shadows. Tears came into his eyes and he angrily blinked them away. No way was he going to let them see him crying.

Pete turned and slouched towards the barn. He wasn't ready to face his parents yet. He climbed into the hayloft and looked out over the field. It was his favourite time of day. The light turned the field into a glowing emerald pattern. The cows' rich red-brown coats shone like jewels in the long slanted bars of light. The dark royal-blue lake was completely still. The hawk — he had looked it up in a bird book and discovered it was a northern harrier — was circling over the trees on the mountain. It must have a nest there.

Finally, reluctantly, he climbed down, shuffled across the yard and went through the backdoor into the kitchen. His mother spotted him first.

"Peter, my little Peter, are you okay, darling? Oh, you're so tall and so brown, oh my goodness, you're limping; we'll have to get you to a proper doctor as soon as we can."

She wrapped her arms around him, and Peter leaned into the hug. She smelled good. She smelled like his mother, a combination of warmth and perfume and safety. He really had missed her. He looked at her. She looked tanned and her blond hair was cut short. She was still wearing her suit coat and a red silk scarf.

"I'm okay," he mumbled. "Rob checked me over."

"Honey, I missed you so much. You know I love you. I just want you to be okay." Her voice was shaky. Was she actually crying?

He only nodded.

"Hey son," said his father. "I hear you've been having quite the little adventure here. You sure scared us. We still don't quite understand what you've been up to. Maybe we'll have time to hear the whole story when we get back to Victoria." He looked around. "Gee, it feels kind of good to be back. Seems like a long time since I was here. Maybe we can all go for a swim before we head back to the city."

Pete stared at his tall, handsome father. His parents looked so out of place. They looked familiar, but Pete felt as if he barely knew them. He mumbled something again. His dad's voice sounded so phony, as if he was just pretending to be happy and underneath he was really mad.

Pete had begged his grandmother not to tell them anything. "Not yet," he said. "I have to figure out what to say."

"But why, Pete?"

"They won't get it," he said. "They'll just be mad. Even with the gold and everything. They'll just think I was stupid."

"What's that?" asked his dad. He turned to Pete's grandmother. "Oh here, Mom, let me get that. You sit down and take it easy. You just got out of the hospital. Here sit in this chair. Put your feet up." His father grabbed the tray of teacups out of Pete's grandma's hands, set them on the table, and then maneuvered her into a chair and slid another chair next to it. He lifted his mother's feet onto the chair. "Just a minute," he said. "I'll get you a cushion."

"Oh, stop fussing at me," she said. "I'm fine. It was just a little, teeny heart attack. Nothing serious."

"That doctor fellow who phoned us seemed to think it was serious. That, and Pete disappearing someplace, now that was serious. I had to interrupt my whole schedule. I'll have to catch up to the orchestra somewhere in eastern Russia."

"I didn't ask you to come," Grandma said. "I know you're busy. Pete here has been looking after me. He is extremely hard-working and competent."

"Peter, look after you? I thought he ran off and got lost. He can barely look after himself."

"Graham, I don't think you know your son very well," Grandma said. There was sudden silence in the room. Pete's dad turned to stare at Pete. Pete stared at the floor. All he wanted to do was go somewhere quiet so he could think about things.

Pete looked around for the door. Maybe it wasn't too late; maybe he could still make a run for it. But then he heard his grandma's voice.

"Pete, come here," she said. He slouched over to where she was sitting in the chair, with her legs propped up and a blanket over her lap.

"How are you doing?" she whispered.

"Okay," he mumbled.

"Later, after dinner, we need to have a talk as a family," she said. "You're going to have to tell them sometime."

Pete stared at his shoes. When he first came, his brand-new sneakers had been bright white. Now they were muddy, torn and falling apart. His friends would laugh if they could see him wearing such ugly shoes. But he kind of liked them that way. They were a souvenir of the summer, a sign of how much he had changed.

"Okay?" she said.

Pete nodded reluctantly.

She took his hand and Pete stood there. He didn't know what he wanted, but he knew he didn't want to talk to his parents. Now they were busy preparing food and getting supper ready.

He went into his bedroom and flopped down on the bed. Words swam around in his head. Although he was bursting to tell his parents what he had done, he wanted it to come out just right. He tried to read a comic book but the words swam together and refused to make any sense. His eyes drooped. He realized he was exhausted. He hadn't slept much the last couple of nights at Bird's house after Rob had taken him home from the hospital, and now the combination of excitement and exhaustion was catching up with him.

When he had arrived at the hospital two days earlier, it was late, way after visiting hours. He had to ring and ring a buzzer to be let in. He knew it would make more sense to go to Bird's house but the person he was most concerned about was his grandma. He had to find out if she was okay — and he had to let her know he was still alive.

The nurse had reluctantly let him in. He had to talk hard to convince her of his identity. Finally he said exhaustedly, "Please phone Dr. Dillon," and while she was gone to phone, he hurried down the hall to his grandmother's room.

She was lying awake in the darkened room. She looked at him and said calmly, "You'd better not be a ghost or I'm gonna get out of this bed and kill you all over again." Then she held out her arms. She kissed him and patted him on the head and said, "You'd better have a good story about this one. Your mom flew back from Africa, but she is waiting for your dad to arrive in Victoria. Then they are driving up together. Rob's been going crazy. I'm just so glad to see you; I'm not even going to yell at you, not just yet."

"But . . . are you okay?"

"I'm fine."

"You're not going to . . . die?"

"Not for a long time. I want to stick around and watch you grow up. You seem to be turning into such an interesting person. At least, you're sure full of surprises. And obviously there are still a few lectures I need to give you."

He flopped into the chair beside her bed and shrugged off his backpack.

"Grandma," he said, "please don't have another heart attack. Because I have something to show you." And then he had taken the heavy leather bag and plunked it on the bed beside her.

His grandmother had opened the bag, looked at the coins in silence, then picked them up and ran them through her hands. She sat there silently for a long time.

Finally, she looked up. Tears were rolling in long shiny streaks down her face but she was smiling. When she spoke, her voice was choked and hoarse, "Whew! Pete, I don't know what to say. You are so amazing. You are totally brilliant. Now tell me the whole tale of your adventures. Where did you go and why? And how on earth did you find these?"

"It was that story you told, how there used to be a town over on the other side of the lake. And in Pierre's diary, he wrote that he won the gold playing poker. He must have hidden the coins in one of the mine tunnels, but he thought the men he had been playing poker with were following him. When Bird read the diary, it sounded like he thought they were out to get him. I think that he thought they wanted to rob him. I guess he never got the chance to bring the gold back to the farm."

"But, Pete, why go in the middle of the night? Why scare us all to death?"

"Because that's when I thought about it. I didn't want to wait. I wanted to give you a really good surprise. I wanted you to be happy. It's all for you."

She stared at him. And then, to his horror, she really

began to cry, loud sobs that he was afraid would bring a nurse running. He sat beside her, frozen, while big, fat tears rolled down her cheeks.

"Pete," she said finally, in a little gasping whisper, "I think you have just saved my life. There's something I didn't tell you." Her voice got a little stronger. "I didn't tell you the real reason I was going to sell the farm. You see, when Jess's dad got brain cancer, he and Fern needed money. They needed money to travel to get treatments. I wanted to help. They're like my other family. So I borrowed money against the farm. I took out a mortgage. I thought I could pay it back. I thought I could manage the payments, but then I got behind. I was embarrassed and, mostly, I was afraid your father would find out. I was afraid he'd get mad again. He would say that I was foolish to borrow money I couldn't pay back. I don't know how much money is in this bag but I think it's a lot. I think it's enough that I won't ever have to worry about money again."

And then he must have passed out or something because when he woke up, he was in another hospital bed, in the same room as his grandmother, and dressed in a hospital gown. After breakfast, Rob came in, followed by the same big cop that had interviewed Pete before.

His grandmother woke up when the cop and Rob came in. Pete told them the whole story. The cop lectured him again about safety and scaring everyone to death and how much the Search and Rescue helicopter had cost the taxpayers, and then they went away and he went back to sleep. Then Fern arrived with Jess and Bird. They screamed when they saw the gold. They demanded the whole story all over again.

They all looked at the gold together, taking the coins out of the bag, counting them, turning them over. They were of many different sizes and types, some silver and most gold. Some had eagles on each side.

"We have to find someone who can tell us what they're worth and where to sell them," Pete's grandmother said. "And we should put them in a bank or somewhere safe. It seems ridiculous to have a fortune in gold sitting in a hospital cupboard."

But that is where they had sat for two days, until his grandmother had been released from the hospital and they had come home together and waited for his parents to arrive. He still hadn't told his parents about the gold, and neither had his grandmother.

—

Now Pete curled up in the middle of the bed, pulled some blankets around his head and shoulders and drifted away.

The next thing he knew someone was shaking his shoulder and calling his name.

"Pete," the voice said. "Peter, come on, wake up, time for dinner."

Groggily, he opened his eyes and tried to unwind the blankets from around his head.

"What time is it?" he asked. He thought perhaps he had slept all night. His head was still full of the dream he had been having. In the dream, he and Pierre had been walking around the farm. Pierre was showing him the new barn, the fence and the house he was building. It was still so vivid and real he couldn't quite believe it had been a dream.

"It's dinner time." His mother's face leaned over him. "Oh Pete, look, you've crawled into bed with your shoes on. I'll have to find you some clean sheets. I wonder where Avery keeps them. And look at your face and hands, darling. You need a good wash. Go get cleaned up. Everyone is waiting for you to come to dinner. My goodness, look at this place, it needs some cleaning. After dinner, I'll make your bed and do your laundry."

"It's my room," he mumbled.

His mother stopped and then she sat down on the bed. "Pete, there's something different about you. You seem like you've grown up this summer. I'm sorry I've been so busy. We haven't really had a chance to talk and we need to talk. All of us together."

Pete didn't know what to say. He looked at her. He wanted her to put her arms around him as she had when he was little and tell him everything would be fine. Instead, he pulled the sheets up over his face. After a while, his mother stood up and left.

Pete got up and stumbled off to the bathroom. His legs still hurt. His eyes didn't seem to be working very well either. When he stared in the mirror, his eyes looked puffy and red, his hair was standing on end, and his freckles stood out like patches of mud on his white face.

He washed and combed his hair and then went reluctantly out to the kitchen.

The dining room table that his grandmother never used was now covered by an amazing amount of food. Pete was suddenly enormously hungry.

He slipped into the only empty chair, next to his father, and began ladling food onto his plate. There was mashed potatoes and gravy, roast chicken, a big salad, sliced tomatoes, homemade biscuits, glazed carrots, and even pizza. He ate lots of everything while around and above him, the adults talked and talked, their voices going on and on like running water or wind and just as meaningless.

"Oh, Graham, be quiet," said Pete's grandmother suddenly. Pete woke up from his daze. What were they arguing about? All he was aware of was that their voices had been getting louder and louder. "Both of you, calm down. And leave Pete alone. He's been through enough. Yes, there is a story and I'm sure it is a long and complicated one. Peter, do you want to tell everyone about it?"

Pete shook his head. He could feel that his face was burning.

"Well, that's okay," said his grandmother. "Because I want

to talk. I think it's time I spoke my mind about all this." Her voice was amazing. It was so strong; it had an edge, like a steel knife. "Graham and Katherine, first of all, I want you to know that having Peter here this summer has been absolutely wonderful. He is such a great kid, and I am very proud of him. Congratulations, you've done a great job raising him. Second, yes, Graham, I have been trying to decide for the last year or so whether or not to sell the farm. I borrowed some money to help my friend Fern when her husband was dying. And then she couldn't pay it back so I couldn't either. She was going to sell her house and I wouldn't let her. The bank demanded the money and so I was going to have to sell for whatever I could get. I contacted a real estate agent to do an assessment to see how much it was worth."

She sighed and took a drink of water. "Well, it turns out it is worth quite a lot. This real estate dealer got very excited. He has an offer from some resort company. I didn't want this farm to be a resort and be covered in houses and a big hotel. Then Pete figured out that I needed money so he undertook to find me some. And this is what he found."

She left the room, and came back with the leather bag.

"Peter has saved my life. I didn't think I was going to be able to survive a move at my age. Losing this place was going to break my heart."

She took out the leather sack and put it on the table, among the dirty plates and leftover food. She opened it up and spilled the gold coins onto the table.

"Our Pete is a very brave and determined young man," she said.

"Oh, my goodness," exclaimed Pete's father. "What is that? Is that really gold? It looks like gold. The lost gold, Pierre's lost gold? You found it. You actually found it." He was stammering in his excitement.

Pete's grandmother lifted her teacup high in the air. "They're mostly American double eagle coins," she said. "And a few other silver pieces. That's what the miners used in the old days. Yes, Peter found it. And a very brave and brilliant job it was too. Here's to you, Peter. You are absolutely amazing. Now please, please tell your parents the story of what you did and how you found it."

His mother and father stared at Pete. "You found this?" his father said. "Yourself?"

"Peter, what on earth have you been up to?" his mother cried. "Was it dangerous?"

"There's an old mine tunnel," Pete said at last. His voice cracked and creaked like a rusty door. "In the gully, up in the woods behind the orchard. A tree fell down in the storm and uncovered the entrance. That's how I hurt my ankle. I fell in a hole. There's a skeleton in there. I think it might be Pierre but the police are investigating that. I found this old black leather thing but when it dried, it turned out to be a map. I followed it, that's why I had to go across the lake. I went to that old ghost town, and I found the gold hidden in a mine. Then the boat blew away and I had to walk home."

It was very hard work getting all those words out but he managed.

"Oh, Peter!" gasped his mom. "I knew this place was too dangerous. I can hardly wait to get you back to Victoria."

"I'm not going," Pete mumbled.

"Excuse me? Speak up, Peter. What did you say?"

"I'M NOT GOING!" Pete said. "CAN YOU HEAR ME NOW? I DON'T WANT TO GO BACK TO VICTORIA!" To his horror, his voice was much louder than he wanted it to be. He tried to bring it back under control but instead it broke like a bad recording.

"You guys are getting a divorce. Where am I supposed to live? Does that mean I get to go back and forth like some stupid toy? You never even talked to me about it. How am I supposed to know what is going on with you? Nobody cares what I think. Nobody listens to me. Nobody!"

He knew he was going to start crying and that would be the very worst thing that could happen. Instead, he pushed back his chair, which fell over with a satisfying bang, stomped to the door, yanked it open, went through it, slammed it behind him and went outside into the cool silent night.

Cousin came running, and Pete leaned over and rubbed his ears. Cousin licked his face.

Behind him, he could hear the door open, could hear his mother calling him, but he knew she couldn't see him standing there in the dark. It sounded like she was crying. He waited. Eventually, his grandmother came out. She sat down on the picnic table and he came out of the dark and sat beside her.

After a while, she said, "Good one, Pete."

When he didn't say anything, she added, "Your mother told me you've done this before, that when you get mad, you can't or won't talk, you just run away."

Pete stared at his feet.

"Pete, that is such nonsense. You can talk. You've been talking just fine the whole time you've been here. You've told me stories; we've talked and argued and laughed. I think you need to give your parents a chance. They love you, and they don't want to hurt you. I think they still love each other, actually, but they're both really unhappy right now. I think you all need to really talk and really, really listen to each other."

"They won't listen," he said. "They never listen. My mom just bosses everyone around and my dad runs away."

"Have you given them a chance? You just assumed that when they came they would be mad at you, instead of proud. You have proved something to yourself this summer. You proved that you are smart and brave and that a lot of people like you. I like you. Bird really likes you."

He stared at her.

"No, she didn't say anything," his grandmother chuckled. "But I've got eyes. I can see. And one more thing. Your coming here made me realize how lonely I've been. And how stupid I've been, locking myself away here, mad at your dad, afraid to talk to him, blaming him for troubles that I had brought on myself and blaming myself for being so foolish. I could have come to visit you more. I could have tried harder; maybe I could have gotten rides with friends. The truth is, I've been a stubborn old fool."

"You're not a fool," he said.

"Sometime in their life, Pete, everyone is a fool. The trip across the lake was your turn. Yes, it turned out okay. But it could have gone wrong. You should have told me what was going on. You should have asked for help. Luckily you pulled it off. But you could have drowned or disappeared like Pierre, and no one would have ever found you. While you were gone, I had lots of time to think, too. And I realized I've been wrong. Nothing is more important than family and the people you love. I've been hiding out here feeling angry and sorry for myself instead of working things out with your dad and your mom. I have also realized that I am getting old and I need help. This place is a lot of work."

"I can help you," he said.

"You need to finish going to school. So I'm going to change my life. It's time. I realize I need to take my own advice. I've always believed there's a solution to every problem if you look hard and you're willing to try. And you proved that's true. So now I know that I want to spend more time with you and your mom and dad in Victoria. First, I need to pay back the bank. Then, if there is some money left over it's going on a new truck, and maybe I'll even hire someone to do some of the chores around here and look after the place when I'm gone."

"Do you know how much the gold is worth?" Pete asked anxiously.

"We have to find someone who can sell it for us. You can't just take old coins to the bank. And the government will want to know about it. They'll want their share. Tomorrow we'll call Rob and ask him to help us."

"But we can keep the farm?"

"Yes, we'll keep it, Pete, my love. We'll keep it forever. Maybe you really will want to live here someday."

"I will," he said.

"Well, wait a few years, sweetie, before you decide. Get an education. You can come here every summer for now. Maybe next year we'll both row across the lake and go explore that old ghost town. Maybe we'll find even more treasure."

"Really?"

"Really. Oh yeah, and I was so mad at you for running off, I spent the whole day in the hospital writing a new poem." She burst out laughing. "Now come back inside," she said. "Otherwise, you and I are both going to be in trouble with your mother. She loves you, sweetie. And you love her, too. It's about time the two of you learned to talk to one another again."

Chapter Thirteen

—

"Wow," Bird said. Jess and Bird were lying on either side of Pete at the beach. Cousin was lying with his head on Pete's feet. "It's amazing how it all worked out, right? It was so incredible when I saw that pile of gold. I still can't quite believe it."

"Pete, tell us again about seeing the monster," Jess said. "Do you really think it is out there?"

"It was just a big wave," Pete said sleepily.

"I've got an idea," Bird said. "Next summer, let's mount a scientific expedition to look for the lake monster. We'll get underwater cameras, and a boat and a microphone, hey, maybe we should learn to scuba dive!"

"I've got a book about the Loch Ness monster," Jess said. "It sounds exactly like the one Pete saw. I'll bet it's out there."

"I didn't really see anything!"

"Maybe you did, maybe you didn't. Remember, no one thought the gold was real until you found it," Bird mused.

"Isn't it amazing what that gold was worth," said Jess. "Imagine, one of those coins was worth almost $1,000."

"It came to about $100,000 altogether," Pete said.

"And imagine Pierre rowing across the lake all the time and winning all that money at poker. Crazy."

"Do you really think that was his ghost you saw?" asked Bird. "I'd love to see a ghost."

"No, you wouldn't," said Pete. "It was freaky."

"It was Pierre's ghost," she said calmly. "I'm sure of it. He was trying to send you a message. He wanted you to save the farm. I'm so jealous," she went on. "I wish I could see a ghost. You got to have all the great adventures without us. But you're coming back next summer, right? So maybe there will be another mystery to solve. Was that really Pierre's body in the cave?"

"No one is sure. They're trying to find his family in France so they can take DNA samples."

"What if they think the gold is theirs?"

"It belongs to me and Grandma because I found it. Grandma says we have to pay some of it to the government."

"Is your grandma going to live in Victoria now?" asked Jess.

"No," Pete said, "but she is going to come for part of the time. She says she might even buy a new truck. Well, maybe. She loves that old truck."

"So what happened with your mom?" Bird asked. "I thought you figured she was going to ground you for life."

"Grandma said we all had to learn to talk to one another, and we had this big family meeting and everybody cried, even my dad. It was so embarrassing." He sighed. "Mom and Dad said we're still a family no matter what. And then my mom said she had underestimated me or something like that and maybe she had been too protective."

Bird and Jess were both staring at him. "Grandma and I are flying to Victoria next week. We're staying with my mom until my dad gets a new place. Then I get to go back and forth. I guess I'll just have to get used to it."

They were all silent for a while.

"C'mon, let's go swimming," Bird said. "Let's not get depressed, just because Pete's going away and it's the end of summer and we all have to go back to stinky old school."

"But next summer is going to be so cool," said Jess. "Because now we know we'll be friends forever! Okay, last one in is a lazy bum!"

They all leapt to their feet and raced into the water. Pete swam out hard and fast, but Bird stayed right beside him. They swam side by side for a while, then stopped, turned over on their backs, lazily stroking to keep themselves going.

"Hey Pete," Bird said, "can I ask you something?"

"Yeah, sure," he said.

"If I email you, will you email back?" He turned to look at her. She was smiling at him. The sun was shining on her wet face and her red hair.

"Yeah, sure," he said.

"Can I ask you something else?" she said.

"Sure," he said again.

"Have you ever had a girlfriend?"

"No."

"Have you ever thought about it?"

"No," he said. He stuck his hot face in the water to cool it off and then flipped his wet hair back out of his eyes. "Yes," he said. "I've thought about it."

"Me and Jess are coming to visit you in Victoria, you know. Your dad gave us tickets to the orchestra. We're coming in October."

"That'll be good," he said. "I can show you guys around. Victoria's kind of a neat place, if you know where to go."

"I'd like that."

They floated side by side, lazily flipping their toes through the green water. Pete watched the shimmer the water made as it slid through his fingers. If he almost closed his eyes, it looked like liquid gold slipping and sliding through his fingers. He turned over, slid under the water, opened his eyes, and then came bubbling up to the surface, spouting like a whale and splashing Bird's hair.

"All right, Peter Eliot," Bird said, "you are in so much trouble. Race you to shore."

And they turned and raced for shore where Cousin was leaping and tossing sticks in the air.

ABOUT THE AUTHOR

Luanne Armstrong is a novelist, freelance writer, editor and publisher. She has written a number of award-winning books for children, as well as novels, non-fiction and poetry. Luanne lives on her organic heritage farm on the east shore of Kootenay Lake. She has Ph.D. in Education, and is an adjunct professor of Creative Writing at the University of British Columbia.

Marquis Book Printing Inc.

Québec, Canada
2008